SHRUNK!
MAYHEM AND METEORITES

3011780084727 5

SHRUNK!
MAYHEM AND METEORITES

F.R. HITCHCOCK

First published in Great Britain in 2014 by Hot Key Books
Northburgh House, 10 Northburgh Street, London EC1V 0AT

A CIP catalogue record for this book is available from the British Library.

ISBN: 978-1-4714-0116-9

1

This book is typeset in 11pt Sabon using Atomik ePublisher

Printed and bound by Clays Ltd, St Ives Plc

Hot Key Books supports the Forest Stewardship Council (FSC), the leading international forest certification organisation, and is committed to printing only on Greenpeace-approved FSC-certified paper.

www.hotkeybooks.com

Hot Key Books is part of the Bonnier Publishing Group
www.bonnierpublishing.com

Bookplate by Kewin and Char

For all children who have ever wanted to write stories

Prologue

Did you know? If you have a shedload of marshmallows, they burn really well, for a really long time . . . with really big flames.

I know that because when it all kicks off, Mrs Worthy makes it right across Mr Burdock's donkey field, onto the beach and into the sea, and her bowl burns like a flare, the whole way.

We're on the first of this summer's 17th Field Craft Troop camps, and Jacob and Eric have been arguing. Or, rather, Jacob's been arguing and Eric's been answering him back like a really wise grown-up.

This has gone on ever since Mr Worthy, our Field Craft leader, announced that he was banning meat sausages and white bread on health grounds, and that, from August, he would be admitting girls. The camping trip to the top of Mr Burdock's donkey field will be the very last of our weekly sausage-fuelled 'boys only' trips.

Jacob hasn't taken either piece of news well – which is how he ended up with the job of lighting the fire. Mr Worthy felt sorry for him, and handed him the matches. Personally,

I would have handed them to Eric, but Mr Worthy's new, he doesn't know Jacob.

I hope we don't all live to regret it.

'Jacob, things have changed. We live in the 21st century. Women run countries, vote, have their own cars,' says Eric.

'But they're girls,' says Jacob, striking the second-to-last match in the box and holding it next to a sheet of smouldering newspaper. 'They won't want to do manly things – like . . . like . . . we do. They'll want to do cutting and sticking.'

I know I should be on Eric's side about girls coming to Field Craft, that would be the mature response, but I'm not that keen on spending every Friday night in the Field Craft hut with my sister, Tilly, her friend Milly and a glue stick. So I keep quiet.

'You, Jacob,' said Eric, 'are in danger of becoming a dinosaur.'

'Dinosaur – me? You're the dinosaur! I'll tell you I'm already prestiged at level 27 on *Dragon Blitz*. Anyway, I'm not going to argue with you two losers.' Jacob lets out a long puff of fury and the smouldering newspaper springs into life. 'Yay!' he cries.

I chuck over a twig and he holds it in the flame. We all hold our breath as the tiny, yellow tongue flicks across the strands of wood. This fire is our only defence against a night of death-by-boredom out here by the sea. Other activities include singing 'One Man Went to Mow', or cooking marshmallows with Mrs Worthy, or both.

The twig lights, and Jacob piles more wood onto the

fire, which doesn't go out. Instead it begins to resemble a respectable campfire. A few minutes more and we might have an almost-out-of-control bonfire.

Other Field Crafters emerge from the shadows to sit near us. Everyone knows Jacob, so no one sits too close.

I lie back against my sleeping bag, listening to the crackle of the flames and the chatter. The sky's turned a delicious midnight blue, and the stars are clear and twinkly. The Worthys might have banned pork sausages and white bread, but they can't ban the night sky.

Eric thumps back onto the ground next to me, while Jacob huffs and puffs at the fire.

'Look,' says Eric, pointing. 'There's Jupiter – just where it ought to be.'

'Where?' I ask.

'Between those two big stars – to the left of the moon.'

I focus on the sliver of moon, and a little to the left, at what appears to be a bright star.

I put my hand up to make an 'O' by putting my thumb and my middle finger together.

'Don't,' says Eric, pushing my arm sideways, so that I can't see my fingers. 'No one would want what happened last time to happen again, would they?'

'I'll kill you if you even think of it, Model Village.' Jacob jabs the fire and the flames light up his face like a demon. 'I do not want to be three inches high, nor do I want the world to end in the next week, because Dad's promised an all-expenses-paid trip to Mega Games World and I'm not missing it.'

I let my hand fall onto my chest. I wasn't really thinking of shrinking Jupiter. Having my own tiny planet was . . . mad, crazy, wonderful, but I wouldn't do it again. It was like being a superhero – except, they don't do stupid things – not REALLY stupid things.

Anyway, I don't have my meteorite; so I can't shrink anything. It's safely tucked up at home.

Sparks from the fire throw themselves up against the clear sky and fade.

I roll over onto my stomach and gaze across the bay towards the town. The castle, normally a dark splodge, is encircled by yellow workman's lights, as if it's wearing a necklace. Underneath me, my belly turns over with hunger.

Mr Worthy appears from the darkness, carrying his guitar, silhouetted against the sky. I can see his baseball cap, sticky-up hair escaping from the gap at the back and the lump behind his neck that's probably the hood of his hoodie. 'Yo!' he yelps. 'Now, dudes, let's pull together around Jacob's fire, and have a musical moment. Mrs Worthy might even break out the marshmallows if we're lucky – all right, Janey, hun?'

'Yuk,' mutters Jacob.

'Yes, Simon,' says Mrs Worthy, like we were all five years old, including Mr Worthy. 'Ready when you are. Marshmallows and tea, coming up in a jiff.'

There's a murmur which might be enthusiasm, but I doubt it.

I shuffle up next to Eric as some of the Hedgelings – they're junior Field Crafters – come to sit by the fire. Mrs Worthy produces a kettle which she hangs over the flames on a long wire attached to a stand and settles a bowl of marshmallows on the ground next to her, handing sticks out to everyone around the fire.

The first chords emerge from Mr Worthy's guitar. It's out of tune. When Mr Worthy starts singing, he's out of tune too.

I close my eyes. It's a shame ears don't have lids on so that you can close them when you need to. The sound's worse when I can't see, so I open my eyes again.

The fire seems to enjoy Mr Worthy's singing, and the flames get stronger, splitting and doubling in size. It actually gives off some heat.

I look up at the stars and wonder how far up the sound can travel. Could someone sitting on the edge of space hear this?

Wheeeeeeeeeeeeee

What's that noise?

Wheeeeeeeeeeeeee

I've heard it before.

Wheeeeeeeeeeeeee

Oh no.

I look up. A shooting star whizzes towards us, a streak of light racing through the sky. A second star slices across the horizon, on a different course, heading towards the town.

BANG.

But I know they're still moving; that they haven't hit anything yet.

'Wish!' yells Jacob.

'Don't,' I say, but my voice is lost.

CLANG.

And then –

THUD.

I think it hits the kettle – the kettle certainly hits the fire.

WHOOOSH.

A fountain of sparks bounces up, showering Mr Worthy and his guitar so that he staggers backwards, brushing himself down in horror. The kettle rolls across the grass, spewing boiling water and steam. Everyone runs, especially Mrs Worthy, who runs fastest. Clutching her bowl of flaming marshmallows, her skirt glowing with embers, she charges off across the field, trailing sparks like a giant firework, all the little kids following, and most of the bigger ones too.

'Wait – dudes – I'll put her out!' shouts Mr Worthy, running for his car. 'I've got a fire extinguisher.' Which is almost exactly when Mrs Worthy throws herself and the marshmallows into the sea.

It leaves me, Eric and Jacob, the remains of the campfire – and the meteorite.

'What was that?' whispers Eric.

'It fell in the fire,' says Jacob. 'Did you wish?'

'Leave it!' I say. 'It'll be boiling hot!'

Around us Field Crafters stamp on spots of flaming grass, people shout, and a team forms to drag a smouldering tent into the sea.

'Ace work, team Field Craft,' shouts Mr Worthy from a safe distance.

Eric pokes the meteorite with a stick, rolling a lump from the ash to the grass where it lies, steaming.

'It's just like yours, Tom,' says Eric.

'Yes,' I say quietly.

We sit staring at the lump of rock glittering in the last scraps of firelight. Behind us two of the Hedgelings are crying, and Mr Worthy's on his phone to their parents.

'Don't touch it,' I warn. 'Leave it alone, or flip it into the sea.'

For one foolish second, I think that's what's going to happen, before Jacob lunges forward to snatch at the meteorite, and Eric leaps to his feet and tries to stop him.

'Mine!' shouts Jacob.

'No!' shouts Eric.

In the dark, I can't see who touches it first, but deep down inside, I know there's trouble ahead.

Chapter 1

It's the following afternoon, and Eric and Jacob are still arguing.

'I got it, it's mine,' says Jacob. 'Look, you can see the burn.'

'That's not true. I've got a burn too.' Eric holds his hand under Jacob's nose.

'Whatever,' says Jacob, emptying the last of a bag of Buttercup Suckers down his gullet. 'Nothing happened – it's not like Tom's meteorite. 'S'useless.'

Eric picks up baby otter and flies him through the air. Baby otter's tiny cloak flares out like a miniature superhero. 'Not necessarily. We just might not know yet. It might be something really weird. What did you wish for? Jacob?'

'Not telling,' says Jacob.

Eric arranges the Woodland Friends badger family into a group around a table.

'Don't tell me,' says Jacob, a look of disgust creeping across his red cheeks, 'you wished for world peace and a box of Woodland Friends.'

Eric's ears flush dark red. I bet he did wish for world peace. That would be just like Eric.

We're in my bedroom, in Grandma's house. Tilly's room is still being repaired after the Jupiter episode. Grandma told Mum and Dad that the roofers she had in must have been shoddy workmen because it was only a year ago that she had the roof repaired and now it was all over Tilly's bedroom floor. Dad had looked confused, but you don't challenge Grandma if you don't have to. Unfortunately, because Tilly's room was almost completely destroyed, I've now got all her Woodland Friends living on my floor. It was either them, or Tilly. Although the Woodland Friends are only four inches tall and made of plastic, I decided they were more fun. Mum and Dad got Tilly.

'I tried your meteorite,' I say. 'I tried holding it and shrinking something – but nothing happened.'

'Perhaps Model Village has lost his magical power?' says Jacob, a smile on his face, leaning back against a landslide of Tilly's soft toys.

'Of course not,' I say, but my heart sinks. He could be right – I haven't actually shrunk anything for ages. I wonder which is more scary – shrinking things, sometimes the wrong things, or finding that I can't shrink things? For a moment, I feel about 1% good.

And then Eric says: 'You haven't, have you, Tom? Could we test it?'

I take a deep breath, and take my meteorite from the bedside table. It's smaller than the one that fell last night and fits neatly in the palm of my hand. 'What shall I shrink?'

Eric picks up a comic. 'This? It can't do any harm.'

I stand back, holding my hand about six inches in front

of my eyes. The comic lying on the bedside rug fits neatly inside the circle of my thumb and my middle finger.

I turn the meteorite over in my pocket and

Click.

BANG!

Chapter 2

Tilly.

'I knew you could still do it!' she says, bursting into the room. 'I knew it.'

She leaps forward and grabs the tiny comic from the floor.

'It's so lovely – so perfect – so completely Woodland Friends. Would you like it, baby hedgehog?' she says, wedging it into the paw of the small plastic figure. 'So now – I'd like more.'

She stands, hands on hips, in the middle of my bedroom.

Eric sits behind her, his mouth open. Jacob's brow lowers, and he takes an imaginary shot at her with an imaginary gun.

'More?' I say.

'Yes – more,' she says. 'More tiny things – more things for the Woodland Friends. They cost loads in the shops, and if I get them from you, they're free.'

'No – Tilly, I promised Grandma I wouldn't.'

'What?!'

'No.'

Tilly's facc twists into a mask of fury. 'WHAT? I'll tell Grandma you just shrank that comic.'

I think about it for a second, do a risk assessment. 'It doesn't matter, she won't mind.'

'I want you to shrink me a horse trough, a bakery . . .' She goes on, listing them on her fingers, ' . . . a load of books, a digital camera . . . a computer, a printer, a working bathroom, some lights, some hot water . . .'

'No,' I say.

'It's not fair,' says Tilly. 'If you made small things then we could all play together.' She reaches out towards Jacob, who pulls back as if stung. 'We could have a huge, wonderful Woodland Friends party, with everything real. Balloons, tiny crisps, sausages, fairy lights, all of it – and we could use all the families at once, the otters, the badgers, the sheep . . .'

'But most things grow back,' says Eric. 'If Tom shrank the bakery, it would grow back in your bedroom. It would destroy it again.'

'So?' says Tilly. 'Better than a stupid planet. Anyway – what about the small things? Crisps, chocolate.'

I shake my head. 'I won't and anyway, you'd have to buy them first.'

Tilly raises her eyebrows then sinks her face into a sad pout. 'You don't love me. If you loved me, you'd shrink things for me.'

It's difficult, but I say, 'I love you, Tilly – of course I love you.'

Jacob erupts into giggles.

'Well, it doesn't seem like it,' says Tilly, stamping her foot. 'You never play with me. You never shrink things, you never do anything I want to do.'

'Anyway – no,' I say again.

Tilly pauses, and looks down at her Woodland Friends. 'You've been messing with my toys.'

'I touched baby otter,' says Eric. 'And –'

It appears that Tilly's hair stands on end. Her head certainly gets bigger and her voice fills the room, so that I step back against the door, and Jacob creeps towards the window.

'NEVER, NEVER, NEVER touch my Woodland Friends,' she shrieks. 'EVER.'

'But you wanted me to make things for them, so that we could all play together.'

She swings round, her eyes wide and wild.

'Yes – I did. But that's different – I GET TO CHOOSE!'

I stand back and wait. She goes still – her body droops, her shoulders sag, but her hands come up in prayer.

'Please shrink things for me, Tom, pretty please.' Her face is all sunshine and roses. She thinks she's irresistible. 'It's my birthday next week . . .'

I shake my head.

'In that case . . .' The sunshine and roses vanish under a thundercloud. 'In that case . . . I will make you suffer for it. I will have my revenge.'

She throws the door open, so that it bangs against the wall again, raises her nose in the air, and stomps out onto the landing, kicking the Woodland Friends as she goes.

'I will have my revenge – and you'll wish you'd never said no,' she shouts. 'By the time I've finished, you'll wish – you'll wish you'd never even been born!'

There's a crash further down the landing as Mum and Dad's door slams.

I close my door gently.

We sit back on the floor, staring at the Woodland Friends.

'Gosh,' says Eric, cleaning his glasses on the corner of his T-shirt.

'Yes,' I say.

'That,' says Jacob, 'is exactly why we can't have girls in Field Craft.' He flings baby otter up towards the ceiling and catches him in a mug of cold cocoa. 'They're too nasty.'

Chapter 3

Dad's working on a new magic trick. He's standing in the garage, surrounded by plywood and black paint tins. He's got a long black box lying on the table. 'It's for your mum,' he says. 'I want to saw her in half.'

'Nice thought,' I say, trying to give him my full attention, but half my brain is actually worrying about Tilly's revenge. Instinctively I stand with my back to the wall. 'Couldn't you start with a rabbit?'

'A rabbit?' says Dad. 'I can't saw a rabbit in half!'

'It's just that rabbits are . . .'

'Shorter?' suggests Eric. He shuffles along the lane, his shoes squeaking. He stops outside the garage door, looking anxious, as if something's bothering him.

Dad does one of those little jumps that people do when they're very excited. 'Eric,' he says. 'Perfect timing, I need an audience. Now, can I try the penny behind the ear trick on you?' Dad reaches into his pocket too fast, and a handful of coins spin onto the floor.

Eric and I grovel under the car, picking them up. 'You've already done it,' says Eric. 'Twice.'

'Have I shown you the floating card?'

'Yes,' says Eric.

'Coin changing into a twenty-pound note?' asks Dad, pulling a long chain of handkerchiefs from his pocket.

''Fraid so, Mr Perks,' says Eric. 'And the bunch of flowers, rabbit in the hat, the sword trick and the dove in the cola bottle.'

'Ah ha! But you haven't seen anyone sawn in half?' says Dad.

Eric shoves his glasses back up his nose. 'Is that a good idea?' he says. 'I mean – how does it work?'

'If you'd like to volunteer . . .' Dad picks up his saw, wobbles it back and forth, and demonstrates just how sharp it is by shredding two of Grandma's geraniums. The tattered leaves float to the garage floor.

We all stare.

'Tell you what, Dad,' I say. 'Why not use one of Tilly's soft toys? They're all in my bedroom. She'd never miss one – and if the trick goes wrong it won't matter. I'll find one.'

Eric squeaks up to the house behind me.

'What's the matter with your shoes?' I ask, stopping outside the front door.

'I don't know. I'm sure they were dry when I put them on, but now they seem to be full of water. I don't understand it. Anyway, that doesn't matter. I came round because of the castle.'

'What about the castle?'

Eric takes off his glasses and cleans them on his T-shirt. 'You know Dad says it's built on the giant meteorite? Well they're digging up the courtyard. They're drilling into the heart of the whole thing, into the meteorite itself. There are men and vans and trucks. Like a building site.'

I push open the front door. Grandma's been baking for the model village cafe again. There are millions of banana scones laid out all over the floor, cooling.

'Do you mean the silvery rock, the glittery one?' I pick my way around the scones.

Eric stops, staring at the scones. 'Yes, exactly. The ancient meteorite. Dad says it's unstable. He says they shouldn't mess with it. That's an awful lot of scones,' he says, leaning down to sniff them. 'Banana! Wow – delicious! Yes, Dad says it could be dangerous, that people don't realise how powerful it is. Anyway, I wanted to ask your grandma about it.' He pauses, rubbing his eyes again. 'I don't always believe my dad.'

'Um, no,' I say, thinking of Eric's mad dad and Grandma, the two weirdest people in the village. 'I think she's down in the model village.'

'That's a shame. I thought she might let me hold the little meteorite again. The one that landed in the campfire. I thought that while Jacob wasn't around, I could see if I had any powers. You did give it to her, didn't you?'

'I did,' I say. I didn't exactly give it to Grandma; she demanded it the moment I got back from the Field Craft camp. She saw it come down, and she asked who had it. When I told her it landed between Eric and Jacob, she shook her head and said, 'That cannot be good'. She saw the other meteorite too, the one that hit Bywater-by-Sea, but although she searched all evening, she couldn't find it.

So long as Tilly didn't get it, I don't care.

Eric squeaks up the stairs behind me. His feet are ridiculously noisy.

'I wonder . . .' But I'm stopped mid-sentence by the sight of Tilly, armed with a cat basket, blocking the top of the stairs. 'What?' I say.

'Mum's taking me to buy my birthday present,' says Tilly.

'But that's next week.'

'Yes, but I want it now. After all, there's not much fun in my life, not since you made a huge hole in the roof of my bedroom.'

'Hi, Eric,' says Mum, appearing behind Tilly. 'We're on our way to the BBS Animal Rescue Centre to see whether they've got anything suitable.'

'A pony,' says Tilly.

Mum's mouth opens and closes. 'Possibly not.'

'A puppy then – I want a Rottweiler or a Germany shepherd, and I'm going to call it Cuddles.'

'A dog?' squeaks Mum. 'I thought a guinea pig or something small. A couple of mice.'

Tilly doesn't actually stamp her foot, but it feels as if she does.

She twists her face into a smile-scowl. 'When I get my puppy, I'm going to train it to eat particular things, Tom. Like pants, and socks, and meteorites.'

'Meteorites? How funny,' says Mum. 'Well, let's see what they have at the rescue centre, shall we? We might have to make do with a gerbil or something.'

Tilly's lip juts out so far that you could balance a book on it, and then she glances across and does her smug face. 'Anyway,' she says. 'Enjoy your bedroom. I said I'd get my revenge. Come on, Mum, let's go and find that puppy.'

Chapter 4

Enjoy your bedroom? My heart sinks. Very slowly I stick my head around the door. A huge pile of nylon fluffy things with plastic eyes fills a corner of my bedroom just as it has since the Jupiter episode. Woodland Friends are strewn across the floor.

Perhaps she's just winding me up.

Eric sits on my bed and takes off his shoes while I rummage around looking for a suitable victim for Dad. Eric pours what looks like a shoeful of water down the basin. 'See?' he says. 'Water, for no reason, loads of it.'

'Borrow my shoes,' I say, pulling Frizzy McBurst, a blue fluffy monkey toy, from the arms of Bun Bun the pink dragon and tossing them across the room.

'Are these yours?' Eric points under my bed.

'Should be. Tilly's clothes are in Mum and Dad's room.'

Eric leans down and pokes at my shoes. 'It's just that they're full of . . . stuff.'

'Stuff?' I say, pulling out a cheetah, a skunk, a blue donkey, a unicorn and something I can only describe as a purple werewolf. They're all too small to be cut in half. 'Like what?'

'Like, worms . . . earth?' says Eric, poking them. 'Oh, and they're glued to the carpet.'

'What?' I say, stepping over to look. He's right; they're brimful of animal life, and I can't pick them up, not without taking Grandma's rug too. 'Mum'll kill me. Grandma'll kill me twice. I mean, what a . . .'

'Tilly?' asks Eric.

I nod.

He wrenches one shoe from the rug. A trail of purple threads hangs from the sole.

'It's not going to make me change my mind,' I say, yanking more soft toys out of the cupboard. 'It's not just that shrinking things can have such huge consequences, it's because it's for Tilly of all people. I mean, honestly – what a waste of a power. I don't want to spend the rest of my life shrinking cakes.'

'Terrible waste of cake, too,' says Eric, kneeling down beside me to trawl through the fur and fluff. 'Don't worry. I'm sure she's got it out of her system. Anyway, what are we looking for?' he says, carefully lining the toys up as if they were real. He strokes a fluffy egg case, laying it between a purple zebra and a nylon snow leopard. On contact with the floor, the egg case pings open, letting out a high-pitched siren, and a small alien dinosaur springs up to bare its furry teeth.

'Yow!' Eric squeals, dropping it.

'We're looking for a kangaroo-monkey thing, with eight arms and a lion's tail. It's called Koyo.'

'It's not here,' says Eric, poking his nose into the cupboard.

I sit back on my heels and study the bedroom. Koyo is

far too big to hide. But something above my head catches my attention. There it is, glued to the ceiling over my bed. A three-foot pink monster, glaring down at my pillow; its eyes mad and round and plastic.

'Eric.' I point at the ceiling.

He looks up. 'Oh, Tom,' he sighs. 'I can't help feeling she's only just begun.'

Chapter 5

We yank Koyo from the ceiling, leaving eight new holes in the plaster, and deliver him to Dad.

'Don't you want to watch?' asks Dad, wielding his saw again.

I shake my head. 'We need to find Grandma.'

Eric's persuaded me to ignore Tilly, although I'd really like to stick her in a pedalo and push her out to sea. Hopefully, she'd never come back. Failing that – I'd get her to eat Grandma's Brussels sprout surprise.

Every day.

We leave through the garage door and blink in the sunlight. Eric's feet must still be wet because he's leaving footprints all along the pavement. He doesn't seem to notice and I expect it to stop, but it doesn't. It's as if he's got a shower attachment in the soles of his feet.

'Ah – it's the wusses.'

A crowd of holidaymakers parts, to show Jacob sitting on a bench set into the wall that surrounds the model village. He's got sweets and his hand jabs into the paper bag every second to get another and stuff it in his mouth.

'Morning, Jacob,' says Eric.

'Morning, Snot Face,' says Jacob. 'Have you thought of a plan?'

'A plan about what?' I ask. 'We were on our way to ask Grandma about the castle. Apparently someone's digging it up.'

Jacob curls his lip in disgust. 'My dad says they're archaeologists, nerds, boffins . . . you don't want to bother with them. The real issue, the issue at the heart of all the . . . hearts in this town – all the hearts that matter, that is – is what we're going to do about Field Craft.'

'Is it?' says Eric. 'I thought we'd discussed this.'

'We did, but now I've got my own plan. A very good, very clever plan.'

Eric glances at me. 'What kind of a plan, Jacob?'

Jacob sticks a Pomegranate Parcel in his mouth and taps the side of his nose.

I stare at him. I'm trying to work out what's going on in his head, apart from sugar and fat. I've never really been able to work out much about Jacob's brain, except that he's probably got one – or, at least, he's got one about the same size as the average pat of butter.

'I've been thinking about the Field Craft troop generally,' he says. 'I think we need to suck up to Mr Worthy.'

'Oh?' says Eric, making wet patterns on the dry pavement.

The pavement must be very hot, because the water from Eric's feet finally seems to be drying up. I'm about to say something when Jacob waves his Field Craft 'Musical Moments' badge under my nose.

'Yes,' he says. 'I think we should join him for a singalong. Show him the benefits of just boys, being boys, together.'

'Ah,' says Eric brightly. 'So that's your plan?'

Jacob shakes his head and lowers his brows. He looks alarmingly Neanderthal. 'My full plan is too fiendish to discuss in the street. Getting to know the Worthys is no more than a softening-up technique.'

With that, Jacob places one end of a grapefruit sour in his mouth and stands up. 'Bye all,' he says, turning away. He jangles the change in his pocket and, humming 'Ten Green Bottles', forces his way through a family of ice cream eaters.

The smallest child's ice cream plummets from the cone and splats on the tarmac.

Jacob doesn't even stop. Instead, he melts into the crowd.

Eric and I search the model village for Grandma, and then, when we can't find her, walk on and spend twenty minutes staring at the castle. He's right. Someone's digging up the courtyard. Noisily, with machinery and drills.

'Is that right? Is that how archaeologists do things?' I ask.

'I don't know,' says Eric. 'I thought they scraped things with small trowels.'

We turn for home, passing the crazy golf packed with families firing golf balls out into the sea. We have nearly reached the model village when our conversation is interrupted by a blood-curdling scream.

'That creature has got to go!' Dad's voice. 'Are you mad?'

We run towards the garage.

Dad's standing on the bonnet of the car, his hammer

raised in the air. Next to him, Mum's looking pained, and in front of them both, Tilly's standing, her face pinched into determination. Behind her, on the floor, is a cardboard box.

'What is it; what's happened?' I ask.

'I got my pet,' says Tilly, her eyes flashing.

'And what is it?' asks Eric.

'You don't want to know,' says Dad, pulling at his collar and smoothing his hair down. 'It's not staying, you know. Your grandmother won't allow it.'

Tilly harrumphs, turns, picks up the box and slides back the lid. 'Eric – Tom. Meet Cutie Pie, my Amazonian, girl tarantula. She's come to live with us.'

Chapter 6

The tarantula didn't even survive the afternoon. Grandma took one look and ordered that it should return to the rescue centre.

'But Grandma,' said Tilly, 'Cutie Pie was my favourite pet, EVER!'

I can't say I was sorry. Dad offered to make it vanish in the new disappearing cabinet that he hasn't built yet, but Grandma looked at him over her glasses and told him not to be silly.

Now Tilly's on the landing, humming. I haven't said anything about the shoes, or Koyo hanging over my bed. I haven't mentioned the chilli powder in my cereal, or the garlic in my sock drawer, and I even kept quiet when she volunteered me at breakfast for Mum and Dad's magic trick on Saturday night. I especially haven't mentioned the note I just found pinned to a tin of chocolate worms on my bedside table: 'I haf taken yur ston. Shrink stuf or els,' and the fact that my meteorite is missing. I'm really hoping that Tilly can't actually do anything with it. Eric tried using it once and nothing happened – and Eric's intelligent. She must have stolen it while I was out with Eric yesterday. It means that nothing is safe any more. The sooner they fix that hole in the roof, the better. If I have to live with Tilly having access to my room for much longer I will not be responsible for my actions.

I'm currently wondering what to do with my sheets. They're covered in dried glue. It's set hard and clear and although I could peel it off, it would take all day. Getting rid of the slugs under my pillow was bad enough.

The door to my room crashes open. Tilly stands in the doorway, her brows pinched down across her forehead. 'So – have you changed your mind?' she barks.

I wrench the sheets back over the bed. They stick out like boards, but I pretend everything's normal.

'No,' I say. 'I absolutely won't do it.'

'OK,' says Tilly. 'That's fine.' She swings on her heel to leave and then stops, one foot on the landing. 'To-om,' she says, her voice turning to sugar. 'Is it true that at Field Craft you have to get up at 3 a.m., and go on a five-mile run?'

I think back. 'I don't remember going on a five-mile run.'

Tilly tilts her head. 'What about clothes? Do you wear horrid yellow boots? And bobble hats, even in the summer?'

I shake my head.

Tilly comes back into the room. She picks up my last Planet Whirl lollipop from the bedside table and tugs at the cellophane wrapping. 'What about Mr Worthy? Is he nice or does he run in and out of the tents dressed in a Frankenstein mask scaring everyone? And is there really a giant insect living in the woods that eats soft toys?'

I grab the lolly out of her hand, just before she manages to lick it. 'Tilly – what are you on about?'

'Nothing. Just something Jacob told Milly. You didn't bother to tell me about it.'

'That's because it's not true.'

'Doesn't matter that it's not true. You didn't tell me. You don't love me enough.'

She gives a long theatrical sniff and sits down on my floor to play with the Woodland Friends.

I stand blinking at her back. I'm speechless. Utterly speechless.

I stand outside in the model village, breathing deeply and wondering what to do about Tilly. I might have to leave home, move in with Eric.

Eric.

Eric's shoes.

I think about yesterday. His shoes, all that water. And then I think about where we were when the meteorite fell. By a campfire, with a kettle – full of water.

I stare down the hill towards the crazy golf. A man shoots a ball into the sea, and another backwards into the model village.

But Eric can't have powers. He hasn't got the meteorite – Grandma's got it.

Unless . . .

Feeling about 61% good, I race back towards the house.

Chapter 7

Grandma's making marrow and ginger jam. There's a cloud of sweet steam pouring out of the door and the radio's on full blast in the kitchen.

'Grandma,' I say. 'Have you got Jacob and Eric's meteorite, safe?'

She wipes her hands on her apron and reaches for the drawer in the kitchen table. 'Yes, dear. Here it is.'

She hands it to me. It's heavier than mine, but smaller. Glittery, like the rock under the castle.

I run my fingers over the surface. There is nothing to mark this meteorite out from the thousands that people have collected across the country, except that I know that, because we're in Bywater-by-Sea, it's different.

'Grandma – do you think it's possible that someone could have powers without actually having possession of the meteorite?'

Grandma stirs the jam. A wave of bubbles races over the surface. 'I don't know – I suppose it must be possible – I hadn't thought. As far as I'm aware, Miss Darling, the green-fingered lady, has her green fingers all the time.' She looks up at me. 'You're worried about Jacob, aren't you?'

I nod.

The business of Tilly stealing my meteorite is nagging at the back of my mind. 'And what about someone else having your meteorite, would they have your powers?'

Grandma shakes her head. 'No – definitely not. They're personalised, so to speak.' She swings round to look at me. 'Why do you ask, Tom?'

After a millisecond of wrangling with my conscience I hand Grandma the note. She reads it twice and laughs. 'That girl! Really, you have to admire her.'

'Do you?' I ask.

'She's clever – very clever.'

'Is she?'

'Oh yes – you mark my words, she's running a brilliant campaign.' Grandma crangs down the stove lid.

I think of garlic in my sock drawer. I wouldn't call it brilliant – more, annoying.

'Anyway,' she says. 'See if you can shrink something without it. Something that won't do any harm.'

'Why don't you?' I ask.

'Me!' Grandma flaps her apron at me. 'I've not done it for years – but you – I bet you've shrunk something recently.'

I look away. The blush creeps over my face. I put my middle finger and thumb together and look around the kitchen for something that won't matter. There's a packet of Dreamy Squidges lying on the table.

They look tiny inside the 'O' of my fingers.

Click.

'Oh!' says Grandma. 'How disappointing. You can't.' I shake my hand as if a tiny packet of Dreamy Squidges might be lurking on my palm, but it's disappointingly empty. 'But that doesn't mean it's the same for everyone. What do you think those boys wished for?'

'Well, Eric almost certainly will have wished for world peace, or an end to war – but Jacob? Flying? Sweets? Shrinking? World domination?'

'Oh dear. Well, you know it doesn't exactly work the way people expect. I wonder what powers they'll end up with?' asks Grandma, sinking to a chair.

I think about Eric's feet. 'The thing is, Grandma, I think Eric might have the power of soaking things. He's gone . . . soggy . . . and he seems to have gone soggy without being near the meteorite.'

Grandma's mouth falls open. 'And Jacob?' she asks.

I think back to the very hot tarmac. The melted ice cream. 'I've got a theory, Grandma, I just hope I'm wrong.'

It's Field Craft at half past five. Mr Worthy's teaching Jacob to play the guitar on the porch when we arrive. The chosen tune is 'Baa Baa Black Sheep'. Fortunately, the Field Craft hut stands on its own on the beach. It's painted hundreds of crazy colours because the last Field Craft leader decided not to invest in paint. Instead, we all brought in pots of leftovers from home. I think the dayglo yellow might have been a mistake.

I've walked with Eric. He's still shedding water; this time it's dripping off his hair. 'Eric,' I say, taking him past a bunch of enthusiastic knot tiers and on to the inside of the hut. 'I've been talking to Grandma, and we've discovered something. Something – surprising.'

Eric pulls his fleece over his head, keeping his hat on. 'You think that some powers work without the meteorite.'

'Yes, how did you know?'

Eric takes off the hat and a single spurt of water arcs high into the air and sprays the pegs, six feet away.

'Oops,' I say. 'Is it like that all the time?'

Eric nods, a single tear creeping down his cheek. 'Although, actually, this morning, my bed was altogether drier than yesterday – so perhaps when I'm asleep I don't leak in quite the same way.'

I think about shrinking Jupiter and nearly causing the end of the world. 'I'm sorry, Eric – yours is much worse than mine.'

Eric shrugs. 'I'm sure it'll have its upside.' He doesn't sound very sure. I want to tell him about Jacob, but we're corralled by Mr Worthy, staggering in from the porch, surrounded by Hedgelings. He clears his throat after his marathon rendition of 'Baa Baa Black Sheep'.

'Boys,' he says, 'in preparation for the arrival of the girls next week, I thought we could do some more feminine activities. This evening it's pipe-cleaner flowers or butterflies for Mummy; bracelet making; and for anyone who's feeling a little more ambitious – papier mâché dragons.'

Mrs Worthy beams out from the kitchen, where she's laid out a feast of pale orange squash and misshapen brown biscuits. 'Fun, fun, fun!' she says.

I glance over to Jacob, whose face is fixed in a smile. He's gripping Mr Worthy's guitar, and I could swear that there's smoke coming out from behind his fingers.

Or is that steam rising from his head?

Either way. There can be no doubt that the plastic chair supporting his enormous bottom is melting.

Chapter 8

The next morning, I have the house to myself and spend it searching. Tilly's at Milly's house, Dad's building things in the garage, Mum's practising card tricks in the garden. I start with my own room. After I've searched the Woodland Friends, I try the soft toys, and finally the sparkly palace. I find mouldy apple cores, and sweet wrappers, but no meteorite. Next, I try Mum and Dad's room, but there really aren't many places it can be. The sitting room's no good, the dining room's a dead loss.

'What are you doing, Tom?' asks Grandma, labelling her jam.

'Looking for my meteorite. I don't feel right without it.'

'I understand,' says Grandma. 'It'll turn up. Don't you worry.'

I only hope she's right.

'I wonder if I have got a power, and just don't know it yet?' says Jacob, plunging his hand into a bag of sweets and grabbing a Rainbow Chew. The sweet dissolves on the ends of his fingers and drips back into the bag, running all over the Fizz Pop Bombs, which crackle as they melt. 'I've tried shape-shifting, flying and – I'm not invisible, am I?'

Eric shakes his head.

'Shame. I really thought I'd be able to fly. Rubbish sweets, these,' says Jacob, reaching for another handful. 'Do you want one?'

We're on the edge of Fairies' Bottom Woods, at the first girls' and boys' co-educational Field Craft camp-out.

Co-educational is Mr Worthy's word.

'Perhaps you haven't got any magic,' I say, glancing at Eric. We've decided that it would be safer for everyone if Jacob didn't know he had a power, although I suppose he's bound to find out in the end. I take something round and sticky from the sweets bag. I put it in my mouth. It's warm and it tastes of . . . mint and melon?

'Yuk – this sweet is disgusting,' I say, spitting into my hand and shoving it into the grass. Eric sprinkles the ground around Jacob's smouldering feet. Small puddles form and evaporate in the blink of an eye. I take another sweet from Jacob's bag. This one seems to be full of chilli because I can only keep it in my mouth for a second before I have to run into the woods and spit it out. I'd swear it was bigger too, larger than when I took it from the bag.

'What's the matter with the sweets?' I ask on my way back over the grass.

Jacob shrugs and Eric takes the bag to have a look inside. He raises one eyebrow. 'They look fine,' he says. 'If a little gooey.'

I spit the last speck of chilli onto the grass. 'Well, they're not. If I was you, Jacob, I'd take them back.'

'Good idea,' says Jacob. 'I'll finish the bag, and take it to the sweet shop. Tell them they were rubbish. They'll give me a lifetime supply of Dancing Mice, you know, the ones that feel like they're running around on your tongue.'

'Really?' says Eric. 'You'd do that?'

''Course,' says Jacob. 'Why not?'

'It wouldn't be morally wrong to take an empty bag back to a shop and demand replacements? You wouldn't feel foolish?'

Jacob stares into space for a moment. 'No. Why would I? Anyway – where are we going to pitch our tent?'

I'd suggested that I go early to Field Craft Camp so that I wasn't at home. Tilly's new hamster, Nightstorm, has had to go back to the animal rescue centre. It bites. Dad had to have five stitches. Tilly's howling, Dad's yelling and the house is not a happy place.

The hamster also ate the curtains, and Grandma went ballistic. So now Tilly claims she's getting a crocodile. Mum said maybe a parrot. I don't personally think she deserves anything. Not until she gives back my meteorite.

Eric had said he'd come with me and he persuaded Jacob on the grounds that leaving Jacob on his own was a recipe for catastrophe. As we were here early, we've had to help Mr Worthy set up the activities. Apparently we're going to do: stargazing, finding medicines in leaves, capture the flag, going for a nature walk and kickboxing, and there will be face painting. Mrs Worthy is practically spinning with excitement and has made a tray of grey biscuits that might, or might not, be cheesy. Mr Worthy keeps saying 'Yo' and burbling about 'gender equality', whatever that is.

Eric sets up the telescope and fiddles with the tracking motor. He's the only one that knows how to work it.

He's also the only one that's looking forward to the girls coming. Personally, I can't think of anything less fun than spending an evening with Tilly and Milly and all their friends.

'Hey, Snot Face! You're looking the wrong way, and it's daylight – dur,' says Jacob, licking the hot sugar from his fingers.

Eric pinches his lips and keeps his eyes pressed against the eyepiece. He's got the telescope trained on the castle. 'Jacob, please be quiet. Tom,' he says, 'take a look at this.'

Chapter 9

I've never looked through a telescope by day; it's like being a spy. Everything over in Bywater-by-Sea is really big, but it must be two miles away. 'What, exactly?' I ask.

'That person to the left, on the castle wall.'

I hadn't spotted her. I think it's a girl, dressed in black with a red thing around her neck, and she's climbing over a pile of rubble out of the castle. She's got a backpack on and she's moving fast. 'Who is she?' I ask.

'More to the point – how did she get in?' says Eric. 'If she can get in, we can get in. We can find out what's going on.'

Jacob points at me. 'You could shrink Snot Face. Let him go on an adventure – a teeny weeny adventure. He could take a Woodland Friend for company. He could take a look inside and . . . and . . . have a tea party.'

Eric ignores him. 'Did you recognise her?'

I shake my head. 'She doesn't look a bit like any of Tilly's friends, she's not . . .'

'Pink enough?' says Jacob. 'It's all going to be a disaster, letting them in.'

Jacob stands and stamps his foot, and a spear of flame

jets backwards from his ankle. It catches Mrs Worthy's barbecue, singeing a pile of beanburgers and releasing a stream of hot cheese that runs out from the bottom of the barbecue and seeps into the grass.

Eric leaps up to pour water on, which means that I'm left to put out the grass and make whistling noises as if this sort of thing happens every day.

Behind the smoking barbecue, a large saucepan pings occasional bits of popped corn out onto the grass. So far as I know, it hasn't been anywhere near a cooker.

Jacob doesn't seem to notice. He just reaches for a carton of milk and pours half of it down his throat. 'Tongue's on fire,' he says. 'Must have been that chilli burger I nicked off a Hedgeling.' He's still holding the milk. He stares into the container, as if there's something alien in there.

'What is it?' asks Eric.

'It's alive – look, it's turning to yoghurt! Aaah!' Jacob flings the milk to one side, and it explodes in mid-air, showering us with tiny specks of almost-cheese.

'How did your morning go?' I whisper to Eric, as we wipe the goo from our green Field Craft shirts.

'It was tough. I couldn't follow him into his house, but I put out fires at the art shop, soaked a red-hot lamp post, put a moat around the model village cathedral and hosed down the veg shop. He was looking at the door handle on the town hall when his mum called him in. It was red-hot. He surely must have seen it. I think it's worse when he's angry and, did you notice, his eyes go red a millisecond before the flames come?'

‘Well, then, we’ll have to keep him calm.’

We look around at the camp. Mrs Worthy has hung lace bunting from the top of her tent to the trees. There’s a neat pile of silver paper with scissors and glue sticks. They’re all slightly singed.

‘That,’ says Eric, ‘could prove difficult.’

Chapter 10

'Meet my new cockatoo,' says Tilly when she arrives. She holds up a white ball of feathers in a cage. 'It's called Giggles – the previous owners got rid of it because it wouldn't shut up. I wanted the iguana too, but Mum wouldn't let me have it. '

'Where's it going to live?' asks Eric, poking his finger through the bars.

The cockatoo stares, disdainfully. 'Ladies' underwear,' it says and picks at something on the bottom of the cage. 'What-ev-a.'

'It's going to live in Tom's room.' Tilly smiles at me, her face almost cracked with smugness. 'It'll get him out of bed in the morning.'

'Not until you give me back my meteorite,' I hiss.

Tilly smiles.

The girls have set up camp on the other side of the fire pit and they're dancing around arranging things. Mr Worthy seems delighted. I don't understand why things need arranging – things at Field Craft have always been random. That's the way we like it.

They've arranged the food and some leaves, and now they're arranging a play with music. Mr Worthy suggested that they might like to write a script. Luckily, Tilly's not doing that bit. Although, she's brought her violin, and Milly's brought hers, so they're practising the 'overture'.

I think, if they don't shut up soon, I'm going to ask Jacob to do something about it. A firebolt, perhaps.

It's almost dark, and I wander over to where Eric set up the telescope. Mrs Worthy's pointing out constellations to a group of girls. 'Can you see the Unicorn?' she says. 'Or the Hot Air Balloon – apparently it only appears in July.'

I slip past and line the telescope up with the sliver of moon hanging over the bay.

'Psst,' says a voice behind me. I don't need to look; I can feel the heat. It's Jacob. 'Don't look through there! Let the girls go first; I've put ink on the eyepiece. Quick,' he says, handing me an armful of assorted objects, including a pair of trainers and some crunchy paper bags. 'Hide these in their things.'

I look at what he's given me. There's also his 'I'm a Genius' sweatshirt and a load of Fizz Pop Suckers, fused together by the heat. 'Why?'

'Whateva! Whateva!' yells the cockatoo from the girls' camp.

'They're mine,' says Jacob, ignoring the bird.

'Yes – and?'

'I'll get you!' yells the cockatoo.

'I'm going to say they've been stolen and then Mr Worthy will search the camp and they'll be found in the girls' stuff.

They'll get into trouble and Mr Worthy'll ban the girls. I'm going to hide my game console and my phone in with them.'

'Happy birthday to you, squashed bananas and stew . . .' yells the cockatoo.

'That bird's going to drive me mad.' Eric appears like a damp shadow at my elbow. 'Is this the fiendish master plan?' he asks, poking at the sweatshirt.

'*If you're happy and you know it, clap your hands . . .*'

'Might be,' says Jacob. 'Anyway – let's get on with it, quickly, while they're singing.'

'Uh – no,' says Eric. 'I don't think so.'

'*If you're happy and you know it and you really want to show it . . .*'

'Come on, Snot Face – it's our only chance.'

Eric sighs. 'It's not only wrong – it's not going to work. Mr Worthy won't believe it. Don't, Jacob. It'll backfire.'

'Money, money – any money for me!' the cockatoo's getting louder.

I nod, sagely, and hand the sweatshirt back to Jacob, plonking the bag of sweets on top.

'So does that mean you won't back me if I put frogs in our tent and blame it on them?'

'You're right; we won't,' says Eric.

'Or leave a paw print outside their tent and pretend it was a grizzly?'

Eric coughs. 'Really?' he says. 'You were seriously thinking of doing that?'

'Look behind you!' screeches the cockatoo. 'There's an alien.'

Eric is, of course, right, although the thought of getting Milly and Tilly and their violins thrown out of Field Craft is profoundly tempting.

'Oh, honestly – you two, you're such a pair of losers. Right, stand back and prepare to be amazed.' Jacob sets off, leaving behind him a pair of smouldering footprints and the stink of burning grass.

We watch him slip behind the girls and rummage in their bags. He ought to merge with the deep shadows of the trees at the edge of the wood, but he's completely visible because of the steady ping of sparks spinning from his head.

'Should we stop him?' I ask.

'I –' But Eric pauses. We both notice a silhouette crossing in front of the fire. 'Who's that?' he asks.

I stare at the figure. 'I think it's the girl from the castle,' I say. 'There's her red scarf.'

We watch as she follows Jacob towards the girls' camp. She's caught in the wafts of steam that rise from his footprints in the dewy grass. She bends down exactly where Jacob bent down and pulls something out, bringing it back towards the fire, and then on, towards us. 'Your friend seems to have lost his sweets in my overnight bag,' she says quietly.

'Whateva! Whateva!' The cockatoo's leaping around in the cage. Jacob picks it up and dumps it behind the tents.

I open my mouth but no sound comes out.

Eric springs to his feet and sticks out his hand. 'Eric Threepwood. Nice to meet you.'

She tilts her head and surveys him. In the gloom I can't see her properly, but she looks older than Tilly, and definitely more grown up. 'I'm Lily – Lily Lee. So you're not part of the plan – with your steaming friend?'

I shake my head and realise that she probably can't see me. 'No – he's . . .'

'Alone . . .' says Eric.

'Really? Does he know that he's . . . ?'

'He doesn't,' says Eric.

'And we'd rather he didn't,' I say. 'If you don't mind.'

'How interesting,' she says.

'I know a secret about you! I know a secret about you! Murder! Murder!' screams the cockatoo. 'Murder most foul – Murder!!!!'

We all stare as tiny sparks leap from the ends of Jacob's fingers, showering down around the cockatoo's cage. For a moment it's just pretty, like someone with a load of sparklers, but then the sparks fall around the cage and catch on the tents – and within a second, the flames lick over the pile of bags, and the entire girls' camp goes up in multicoloured flames, fireballs shooting up against the sky. Jacob, silhouetted against the blaze, tears towards us, holding something flaming in his hands.

'Fail! Fail! Fai— Epic Fail!' yells the cockatoo, flapping its wings and sending the sparks in wilder and wilder circles.

Eric runs towards the tents and grabs the bird, arcs of water already hitting random objects around him.

'No!' shouts Jacob, a huge column of flame bursting out from the top of his head, his eyes glowing red. 'NO! NO! My Game Cube – my phone! NO!!!'

Chapter 11

We're at the crazy golf hut.

Eric and I were volunteered by Grandma to do the lunchtime duty. I agreed because I've searched every scrap of the house for my meteorite, and now I'm going around searching the same places over and over again. I may have to kill Tilly.

Here, all we have to do is hand golf clubs over the counter, read out the rules and take the money. It's relaxing, really.

I've got a good view of the town from the hut. There's a haze in the air, sort of dusty and glittery, and I notice that over the sweet shop there's a small purple cloud. I'm about to point it out to Eric when a golf ball clatters through the hatch onto the floor. Everyone loses their golf balls on the first hole. No one can do it. It's practically impossible to shoot a ball into the basket of a hot air balloon, especially when it keeps blowing in the wind. So they have to buy another. It's one of Grandma's money-making wheezes.

'One pound please,' I say to the red-faced man, and hand him a new golf ball. He looks ready to argue, but his son drags him away.

Anyway, being here is much nicer than being in the house with Tilly and her cockatoo. The stupid thing spent the whole night shouting: 'Tom did it! Tom did it!' I am going to have to put it in Dad's new disappearing cabinet once he's built it.

What isn't so good, is that Grandma gave us a packed lunch.

'Do you fancy the onion quiche? Or the pea sandwich?' says Eric, holding up a small paper-wrapped parcel seeping dark brown juice. I notice he's barely dripping this morning. His flip-flops are damp, but not wet.

'What's the sauce stuff?' I ask. 'Have you stopped being wet?

Eric licks his finger. 'Prunes – I think they're supposed to go with the quiche. And I've discovered this . . .' He holds out his hand, and a waterfall crashes onto the wooden boards of the hut. 'But when I do this . . .' He points one finger, and a tiny squirt of water shoots across the room and leaves a damp dribble on the wall. 'It seems I can control it.'

'That, my friend, is awesome.' I wonder whether Jacob will be able to develop the same self-control. I doubt it. 'Anything for pudding?'

Eric pokes around in the carrier bag. 'Pie – apple pie – but, oh no, she's not peeled the apples very well.'

'Maggots?'

Eric nods and I reach under the counter for the secret supply of sweet and sour Mango Cheese Balls that Dad hid there and thinks I don't know about. They're better than Jacob's sweets, they don't behave oddly. My hand touches something hard, and very familiar. My meteorite.

'Yay!' I say, pulling it above the counter.

'Definitely yours?' asks Eric.

'Oh, yes,' I say, stroking the ridges of the stone. Warm relief rushes through me. I hadn't realised just how anxious I felt without it. I hold the meteorite in one hand and stuff a Mango Cheese Ball in my mouth with the other. Heaven. I feel so much better now, I can even stop hating Tilly.

I shrink an experimental cheese ball and it ends up about the size of a peppercorn. I tell myself that it's just a test, that really, my power should only be used for good purposes. Saving people, planets, that sort of thing.

That's precisely why I won't give in to Tilly.

That, and her being the whiniest, most objectionable person in town.

My teeth are still embedded in sticky cheese when Jacob appears at the crazy golf window, beaming, dressed in black, wearing a strange harness thing, that might be some sort of utility belt.

'What are you looking so happy about?' asks Eric.

'Dad's agreed to buy me a new Game Cube AND a new phone.'

'How come?' I ask. No one would ever buy me either, certainly not twice.

Jacob sniffs and scratches his bum. There's not the faintest hint of heat coming off him this morning. 'I don't know. I was using Dad's new tablet and it sort of . . . burst into flames. So Dad just said he'd go straight out and buy me a new mega version with *Revenge on Fruit 2*.'

I glance at Eric. 'When you say burst into flames . . . ?'

'I don't understand it; it must have been faulty. But wasn't last night brilliant? The way that spark leapt out of the fire and into the girls' camp?' Jacob grins.

'Is that what happened?' says Eric, poking Grandma's apple pie.

'Brill,' says Jacob. 'Couldn't have planned it better. Now they'll never come back. So, the castle? Are we planning a raid?'

'I suppose so,' I say, looking at Eric. I'm not sure we were planning a raid – and I'm not sure were thinking of doing it with Jacob.

'Right,' says Jacob. 'The castle – fortified, designed to keep us out – well . . .' He points at the crazy golf course. 'We could dig a tunnel?'

Eric and I stare at him.

'OK,' he says, 'We could climb over the roof, using a ladder you shrank, and . . . a snake?'

'A snake?' I ask.

'Ah – boys!' It's Dad. He's come to relieve us but he's carrying two large sheets of plywood speckled with glittery dust. He dumps them against the side of the shed. 'Thanks for standing in. Where are you going now? You wouldn't like to lug my plywood back up to the house would you? I got it out of the skip by the castle. The archaeologists obviously didn't want it. Perfectly good – shame to waste it. Just the thing for the disappearing cabinet.'

'No,' says Jacob. 'We wouldn't. Bye-ee,' he says, heading out past the balloon. 'C'mon, Snot Face, Model Village. Keep up.'

Chapter 12

We leave the golf course and head down towards the castle. Jacob ducks behind a lamp post.

'What are you doing?' I ask.

'Shhh,' he says, holding his finger in front of his mouth. 'Don't want to be spotted.'

I walk down the middle of the road with Eric. No one's looking at us, but plenty of people are staring at Jacob.

'Hey –' whispers Jacob, lurking behind the Air Sea Rescue Helicopter collection box. 'We could borrow the stuff from this lot and climb the walls.'

Eric looks across at him. 'Can you rock climb?' he asks.

Jacob shakes his head. 'No – but it can't be that difficult. My uncle does it and he didn't go to university. Anyway, I've got a grappling hook on my belt.' He waves something the size of a small fish hook.

'Jacob, it wouldn't hold you for a millisecond,' says Eric. 'It's just not possible.'

Two unmarked vans are parked outside the main entrance of the castle, blocking the drive. Eric and I squeeze past and behind us the sound of soft belly on metal demonstrates that it is possible to put something very big through a very small space. Beyond the vans, someone's built a tall fence of corrugated iron with a solid-looking wooden door. There doesn't appear to be any camera system watching us.

'How did that girl Lily get in and out?' asks Eric.

Jacob shrugs and helps himself to a Devil Weevil Candy. He doesn't offer any to us.

I'd like to ask Jacob just to burn the door down, but we're still keeping quiet about his abilities. How he's ignorant of what he did last night I don't quite know – but then Jacob is ignorant of lots of things.

Eric examines the door. 'I've brought this,' he says, pulling a long cardboard tube from under his jacket, long enough to see over the huge fence. On the bottom he's taped an old digital camera, on the top, a mirror. 'A periscope, of sorts.'

Jacob laughs. 'You're not serious – are you?' he says. 'That thing wouldn't last a second.'

'Good idea,' I say quickly, as Eric's face clouds over. 'But maybe I could . . .'

'You could shrink it, Model Village,' says Jacob, leaving smouldering fingerprints on the door. 'Shrink the door.'

I glance at Eric.

He shrugs. 'I don't think it's morally wrong. And I don't think it'll affect anything if you do shrink it. You're not going to put the cosmos out of line, and I won't tell your grandma.'

I look at Jacob.

He picks sugar from his teeth. '*Moi?* I'd never tell, you know me.'

I raise my eyebrow at him.

He shrugs. 'As Snot Face says, it's only a door. Hardly breaking news.'

He's right – it is only a door. I step back five paces, put my middle finger and my thumb together to make an 'O' and hold it up in front of my eyes.

Click.

The door has gone from the fence, and instead, I've got it in my hand, but now it's tiny. I look up to see it had been covering the dark entrance to a tunnel stretching downwards into rock.

'That's odd,' says Eric. 'It should be a cobbled driveway with birds and flowers – what's going on?'

We stand where the door used to be, and I put the tiny door back, so that when it grows it'll be in roughly the right place. Glittering tunnel walls twist downhill; light from some distant bulb reflects from the shining rock. By our feet, inches of fine glittery dust form a dark mat. I put my foot on it. It's soft, like volcanic sand. 'There could be guards,' I say. 'I think we need to disguise ourselves.'

'I am disguised,' says Jacob, flexing his shoulders.

'You're not,' I say.

'You're just wearing clothes that you don't normally wear,' says Eric. 'Technically, that's not disguise. Disguise is when you camouflage yourself in some way, to blend with your surroundings. Or dress up as something in particular – like in Bywater-by-Sea, that might be tourists.'

'Yes,' says Jacob. 'Let's dress up as pensioners and pretend we got lost from a coach trip. Honestly, Eric, what kind of twerp would believe that?'

I look at Jacob. I can't think of anything remotely convincing that he could possibly be – except maybe a wall.

A wall. 'That's it,' I say. 'We could disguise ourselves as part of the tunnel. It's a brilliant idea.'

'Is it?' asks Jacob.

Eric looks at me as if I'm hiding something from him. 'A wall? How?'

'Look,' I say, scooping up a handful of the black dust and smearing it over my arm. It's almost like powder paint – thick enough to cover me and my T-shirt until we become the same colour as the walls.

Jacob and Eric stare as if I'm mad, then reach down and smother themselves with the dust until all I can see are Eric's glasses, Jacob's bag of sweets and the glittery stripes on Jacob's trainers.

'Ready?' whispers Eric, and we follow him into the darkness.

Chapter 13

I go first.

I press my back against the wall, and listen. Behind us seagulls chatter; in front, nothing.

We creep thirty paces down the tunnel. Now I can't hear the sea at all. The sound of our feet is muffled by the glittery dust, so I can't even hear Jacob and Eric.

I'm not sure how I ended up doing this. I'm not sure I like it.

The first light is in an alcove. Where it shines, the black rock looks as if it's made of metal, not stone.

'Wow,' says Eric.

I move on down the corridor. Ahead of us I'm starting to hear drills.

'Aliens,' mutters Jacob. 'It's going to be aliens. They're going to be purple, and they're going to force us to dig for rubies.'

WHOOSH!

A flash of light ahead in the tunnel, and tiny red sparks shoot towards us.

'Duck!' I yell. The red thing pauses, and whizzes around

our heads, spinning faster and faster until it bursts into rainbow colours and disappears. I'd like to scream but I don't think it's going to make any difference.

'Whoa!' whispers Eric.

'Whoa indeed.' I inspect the floor of the tunnel to see if there's anything there, but the rainbow lights have left nothing behind.

'See?' says Jacob. 'I said they were aliens.'

'Don't be silly,' says Eric. 'It must be the effect of drilling on the rock. Dad said it would be dangerous. It must ignite it.'

We creep on, passing more tunnel lights set into the wall. It becomes hotter, and there's another flash of light and more sparkling things whizz past us, but this time they don't stop and they don't turn to rainbows.

I think I've probably stopped breathing.

At the fourth light I find a door in the side of the tunnel. It's old and wooden, and unlocked. It's got a handwritten label: 'Grade A'.

'What do you think? Should we go in?' I whisper.

Eric stands motionless. I imagine he's thinking, but as it's dark and his face is completely covered in black dust, I can't tell.

'Oh, for goodness' sake, stop calculating the probability and let's get on with it,' says Jacob, shoving past. He pushes open the door and we all three look inside. It's a huge cavern, hollowed out of the rock, with hundreds of coloured plastic tubs inside. In the tubs are chunks of stone; above them on racks of metal shelving, glass jars with different grades of dust, from something the size of

Grandma's brown rice to something the size of meatballs. Everything's labelled.

'Megatite?' says Eric. 'I've never heard of that.'

'Quan-ton-i-um Met-e-o-ri-ca, and Los-tel Mon-o-gi-tus,' reads Jacob.

'No rubies, then,' I say to Jacob.

'I still say aliens,' he says. 'They're stealing the planet, stone by stone, and it's up to us to stop them.' He crouches down and creeps back around the door to the tunnel. We pass three more doors in the side of the tunnel, each with a different grade marking, and then the tunnel turns back on itself.

It narrows; three steps descend to a white boarded-out passage. I stop. I don't feel 100% good about going in. 'It's a portal to another world, or the future,' says Jacob. 'And I'm going through it.' He pushes ahead, but Eric grabs his elbow.

'Don't, Jacob, we could be in . . .' But I don't get to finish my sentence because two security guards – one clutching coffees, the other a newspaper – appear behind us.

Chapter 14

'Hey!' the bigger guard shouts. 'Who are you? What are you doing down here?'

'Quick!' shouts Jacob. 'Shrink them!'

'I mustn't,' I say, stepping back against the wall. 'Eric?'

The big one strides forward.

Eric sticks out his hand and a feeble trickle of water runs down his arm, splatting into the glittery dust below. 'It's not working . . .' he says.

'What you playin' at?' says the big guard, reaching out towards Jacob.

'No!' shouts Jacob. His eyes flash and a spit of flame jumps from his hand onto the security guard's trouser leg.

'Yow!' screams the man.

'What?' says Jacob, looking at his hand. In this gloom, there's no way of pretending it didn't come from him. There's no fire anywhere else. 'Was that me?'

Stumbling backwards, the small security guard pours the coffees over his friend.

Jacob sticks out his arm and sends another bolt of fire, this time hitting the small man.

'OW!' shouts the man, throwing himself to the ground while the big one, dripping coffee, whacks the flames on his friend with his newspaper.

Eric waves his arms around creatively, but all he can muster is a few drops.

'This is great!' says Jacob, pointing his hand at the men again.

'NO!' shouts Eric.

And nothing happens.

Jacob points his finger again and again, but no more sparks fly – nothing comes out of his fingertips. 'What?' he says.

The guards are still frantically dabbing at themselves, squashing out sparks.

Eric raises his hand and this time a torrent of water shoots out, snuffing the embers.

The guards pull themselves to their feet and back away up the tunnel. 'You complete nutters,' says the big one.

'Keep away from us,' says the little one.

Jacob lifts up his hand once again, and the guards turn and flee.

Chapter 15

'That was fun,' says Jacob, pointing at things all the way back up the tunnel. From time to time a flame or a spark flies from his fingers but, more often, nothing happens at all. 'But my mouth really hurts, like I've eaten a vindaloo and then drunk a glass of iced water – ow!'

'I don't understand,' says Eric as we emerge from the entrance into the daylight.

'I think I do,' I say.

Eric turns to me. He's got dust all over his glasses. I'm amazed he can see anything at all.

'I think,' I say, 'that our powers were short-circuited by being inside the rock. They became unreliable. That's why Jacob could set fire to things, some of the time, and you had water, some of the time.'

'You two don't seem very surprised by this,' says Jacob, flashing sparks at the skip and sending the whole thing up in flames. Eric immediately douses it, and we walk on towards the vans, leaving a smouldering trail behind us.

I decide not to answer. Eric obviously does too because he changes the subject. 'So now we know what they're doing, but we don't know who or why?'

'You can't get off it that easily – are you telling me that Snot Face here goes all watery?'

'Sort of,' I say.

'And I go fiery.' Jacob crackles, his eyes flash red and a small bush bursts into sparks. 'Ow! That mouth thing again.'

'Just about,' says Eric.

'But is that,' says Jacob, 'because the meteorite went into the fire and knocked the kettle over?'

'Yes,' I say. 'Probably.'

I can see the cogs in Jacob's brain turning over and I wait for the next question.

'So the meteorite landed in a mix of fire and water.'

'Yes,' I say.

'Like your meteorite landed in the model village.'

'Yes,' I say.

'Which is why you can shrink things.'

'Yes.'

Jacob raises his eyebrows while he internally digests what he's discovered. 'OK – I've got that. So what are they doing down in the tunnel?' he asks, turning his pocket full of Sherbet Frazzles into instant and marginally burned candyfloss.

'Mining,' says Eric. 'They're supposed to be scientists, but I don't think that room full of rock looked like samples – it looked more like merchandise.'

'So they're selling the castle rock?' I ask.

'Why would anyone want it?' asks Jacob, taking a large mouthful of the melted Sherbet Frazzles. 'I mean, it's just rock – isn't it?'

I glance at Eric. I don't think the castle rock is just rock. I think Eric's dad is right, that the castle is built on a giant meteorite that fell millions of years ago, and that it could have massive power.

Eric brushes the dust from his arm and looks at it carefully, as if it might be full of tiny alien microbes. I wait for him to say something super intelligent, but he just says: 'Hmmm', and 'I wonder.'

'Hello there, boys,' says a voice from between the vans. 'What are you doing here?'

It's the girl from the camp-out – Lily Lee.

'I . . .' says Eric.

'We . . .' I say.

'Nuffin',' says Jacob, his jaw welded shut by the melted sugar.

'What are you doing here?' I ask.

'Oh, my dad works here. He's Professor Lee and he's heading up the team of scientists. He's sampling the rock.'

Chapter 16

'Get on with it, then,' says Tilly, her grin sliding from smug to delighted.

She's holding out a pile of sparkly fabric.

'Pants! Ladies' underwear!' screams the cockatoo from its cage.

We're behind the curtains on the stage at the town hall. At the back are all the pantomime costumes ever worn and Tilly's been having a ball rustling through them while Mum and Dad crash around decorating the stage along a solar-system theme for the night of 'magical mayhem' to come. They've stuck paper stars and planets all over the walls.

It looks awful.

'A tutu? I'm not wearing that,' I say, opening the curtains a little and peering out at the hall. It's filling up; families drift into the seats. I glance around to see who I recognise. There are loads of people from school. I wish they'd all go away.

Mr and Mrs Worthy come and sit in the front row looking keen. Mr Worthy's got a notepad, as if he's going to learn some techniques from Dad. I could tell him now, they won't be any good.

'These?' Tilly nudges my back with a pair of white rabbit ears.

I ignore her. Jacob, Eric and Eric's dad come in and sit near the front. Jacob's eating Sphinx Bursts straight from the tube. Did he have to come? I scan the seats to see who else I'm going to have to avoid for the rest of the summer.

There's Lily Lee, sitting by a man I've never seen before. Is that Professor Lee? I'd thought he'd be in a lab coat with nerdy glasses and wild hair. But he doesn't look like that at all. He's wearing jeans, he's bearded, and he seems quite ordinary – apart from the safety goggles on his head. But I suppose that's quite ordinary for someone who steals rock.

'Tom,' says Tilly. 'Would you like to change your mind? Will you shrink something for me? Or shall I make Mum make you wear this?' She holds out a skanky hot-dog costume. 'Or this?' An orange mushroom hat with big eyes on the top. 'Or even this?' A monkey suit. She smirks and flounces back to the pantomime rail, humming.

I'd imagined that I could dress like Dad, in a black tail suit with a flower in my buttonhole. But that obviously isn't going to happen.

'Tom did it! Tom did it!' yells the cockatoo.

I peer back through the curtains. Professor Lee is holding something in his hands, flipping it between one palm and the other.

I stare hard. For several minutes.

A meteorite, he's holding a meteorite. Not the shiny rock mined out of the castle, but a stone that's fallen through the atmosphere, singed and rounded by friction.

I study it again, in case I'm wrong. But I'm not, it's a meteorite.

Oh no – I really need to talk to Eric about this.

'Tom!' Mum's voice from behind me. 'We've run out of time – you'll have to wear this. They're all the rage – or at least they were last Christmas. You'll look great.'

She crams me into a leopard-print onesie studded with moons and stars. 'Tilly, quick, the face paint.'

Tilly plasters my face with red and yellow paint and makes me look like a pizza. 'Nice,' she says, with a smirk. 'Very nice.'

And the curtains open.

Chapter 17

Drifts of dust and cobwebs from the ancient curtains float over the audience and we all cough, although half the audience manages to snigger between coughs.

'Welcome, everyone,' bellows Dad.

Tilly's wearing a horrible smug T-shirt that says, 'Daddy's little magician.' She curtseys to the audience. 'Ahhh', they say.

'Tom shrinks things! Tom shrinks things!' screams the cockatoo from its cage.

'My son, my daughter,' says Dad – and he waves his hand across the stage. 'My magic!'

I swallow. I'm caught between extreme embarrassment, and considerable anxiety. It's an unhappy place.

'Shrink!' yells the cockatoo.

Someone from the audience shouts, 'Yes – what the parrot says, shrink something!' Was that Professor Lee?

'Tom shrinks!' screams the cockatoo. 'Bumreek!'

I swallow and stare out into the bright lights trying to work out where the voice comes from. Eric wouldn't heckle, he's too polite, and Jacob doesn't sound like that. Tilly gives me a kick. 'Go on,' she hisses. 'I dare you.'

'Shrink? Oh, my good man, no matter what the bird says, that's . . . not possible,' says Dad, rubbing his hands like he does when he's uncomfortable. 'But *vanish*! Now, that's what we have in mind today! And now, let us get on with the show.'

Mum twirls onto the stage in a pink and yellow cardboard tutu that's supposed to represent Saturn's rings. The tutu gets in the way as she opens up the new enhanced disappearing cabinet. Enhanced because Dad used the glittery dust-covered plywood he took from the skip outside the castle to build it.

I'm not sure it was a good idea to use the plywood. I can't quite put my finger on it, but recently things in Bywater-by-Sea have been even odder than usual. Only last night, Dad started speaking German. And Mum replied in Portuguese. They're both rubbish at languages, but they held a conversation for twenty minutes. In the end, Grandma told them to belt up and switched on the telly.

And that was weird because on the local news, there was a woman who claimed her cat could sing the national anthem, and the man from the Chinese takeaway said that everyone had ordered nothing but lasagne every day for the last week and it was driving him nuts.

'So, a volunteer. Sir, at the front here, the gentleman who asked about shrinking something, would you like to be first in?'

Someone coughs. 'No thanks,' he says. This time I'm sure it is Professor Lee.

'Very well, let's start with one of my daughter's most

treasured possessions. Tilly, please . . . baby otter Woodland Friend.' Tilly hands it over to Dad, who hands it to Mum, who puts it in the disappearing cabinet.

'And three times round, family Perks,' says Dad, pacing around the cabinet. Feeling honestly as if I'd rather be dead, I follow Tilly around the cabinet. From the hall I hear Jacob's laugh and think dark thoughts.

'And . . . open the door, Tom, if you would.'

I open the door of the cabinet and peer in.

Baby otter has gone. I go around the side of the cabinet, trying the other doors.

'It's gone,' I say aloud. 'Baby otter's really vanished,' I mutter to Dad.

'I know. Brilliant, isn't it,' says Dad out of the corner of his mouth. 'It actually works.' He turns back to the audience. 'Voila! Vanished,' he bellows with a flourish. 'Now let us try something bigger. Tilly – the bird, if we may.'

Tilly takes the cockatoo from its cage and for a tantalising moment, it stays sitting on her hand, sweet as Jacob's pocket linings.

'Pump, lump, something gump!' it squawks, then takes off and flaps over the audience, landing once on a tinfoil model of the moon, but settling finally in the eaves of the town hall.

'Ah,' says Dad. 'The cockatoo seems to have already disappeared . . . Ha!' he laughs, chortling at his own joke. 'Anyway, let's have a vanishing volunteer.'

'You mustn't,' I whisper. 'If we don't know where things go . . .'

Dad ignores me. 'Someone? Anyone?' he says. 'Would anyone like to step forward? Who would like to go on the adventure of a lifetime? Disappearing from here, and ending up – who knows where?'

There's a long painful silence, shattered only by the sound of the cockatoo pooing onto an empty seat below.

I'm praying that nobody volunteers, that Dad has to use a rabbit or a dove.

But from the end of one of the rows of seats, someone stands and starts to shuffle through the audience.

They stumble forward out of the gloom towards the stage.

It's Eric's dad.

Chapter 18

'Colin,' says Dad. 'Great – ready to be disappeared?'

'Cosmic,' says Eric's dad.

I look out into the audience desperate to make contact with Eric. I can see his specs reflecting the light but I can't work out if he's looking at me. I wave at him.

There's a giggle from the audience.

I wave again.

A slightly louder giggle ripples through the rows of seats and one or two people wave back.

'Tom,' says Mum, tapping me on the shoulder. 'Shhh.'

'But, Mum . . .' She holds her finger over her mouth. I turn and watch Dad and Eric's dad examine the disappearing cabinet. I've got a rising sense of panic, but I can't think how to deal with this.

'So, Colin, you do know that this disappearing cabinet does actually make you disappear?'

I'm aware of something at the corner of my eye, something moving, but I can't quite see where it is. When I look around to find it, it vanishes.

'I'm cool with it,' says Eric's dad, shuffling his feet and

grinning. 'I might get to go on an intergalactic cruise, find the fourth dimension.'

Dad tilts his head. 'Y-es,' he says, slowly. 'You might.'

'Or,' says Tilly, putting on her most sickly sweet voice, 'he might go all the way to Hawaii and end up with a grass skirt and a coconut bra, dancing on the sands. I expect that's where baby otter is.'

Dad glares at Tilly, and opens the door to the cabinet.

I can't shake the feeling that there's something moving somewhere on the edge of my vision. It keeps catching in the stage lighting and then disappearing.

'Now, what you've all been waiting for . . .' Dad bellows and slams the door to shut Eric's dad inside the cabinet.

It stops.

Everything stops.

It goes dark, then light, then dark and when the lights come on again, it judders. Like a badly edited film. I feel as if I've missed a bit. Perhaps I fell asleep for a second, had a miniature dream, one that lasted a millisecond. But I saw Eric's dad go inside the cabinet, I'm sure of that, then again, I'm almost sure I saw him come out. But it's foggy and I'm still shaking my head and trying to make sense of it when Dad steps forward, blinking.

'Gosh, ladies and gentlemen,' says Dad. 'That was – unusual! Let's hope the electrics are all right.' Dad laughs. No one else does. I shoot a glance at the audience – they all look as if they're in a state of shock, mouths open, staring at the stage.

'Can we have another volunteer to examine the box?'

I stare hard at Eric – but it's Professor Lee who comes up to the stage. I notice he's not holding the meteorite, although he's still got the safety goggles on his head. He looks mildly cross, as if this is a terrible waste of his time. He wrenches open the door, and instead of Eric's dad, a mountain of Brussels sprouts rolls onto the floor.

Chapter 19

We fetch Grandma from home, and spend the rest of the night looking for Eric's dad around the village. It's like when he went off riding Jupiter, but worse, because at least that time we knew where he'd gone.

'He won't be far away,' says Grandma.

'He could be on Mars,' says Eric. 'Seriously – he could. I bet they don't sell prawn crackers on Mars – he won't survive without them.' Eric almost never makes jokes; only when he's desperate. I think he might cry.

'Shh, now. I think he'll be in the village somewhere,' says Grandma, although she doesn't sound convinced.

The moon's very bright tonight, and the whole town's covered in a curious shimmer, like someone's emptied a pot of fairy dust over it.

'So, Scaredy Cat Model Village,' says Jacob, addressing me. 'Not only did you nearly destroy the planet, but your dad has now started to pick off individual members of the population – people like you shouldn't be allowed to have powers.' His flip-flop slips off his foot and he stamps it back on again, releasing a sheet of flame that leaps over the duck pond. The water evaporates, and the scorched ducks take off from the steaming mud, squawking.

'Ow,' he says, spitting. 'I hate that burning thing in my mouth.'

I stare at the un-pond and the homeless ducks. I'm glad that something uncomfortable happens to him when he uses his power, but I can't help wishing that Jacob was two inches tall again. It was nice. Very nice.

'I don't think it's really Mr Perks's fault,' says Eric. 'It's the plywood, isn't it – it was from the skip at the castle.' Eric raises his hand as if he was in class and bursting with something to say. 'Actually, haven't you noticed all the other weird things that are happening around the place?'

'Yes,' I say.

'What d'you mean, weird?' asks Jacob.

'Look,' I say, pointing at Tilly's cockatoo. It's following us down the street – suspiciously quiet. 'It's hard to see at night, but the stupid thing's turning pink.'

'And the eggs,' says Eric. 'There are hens' eggs under every bench.'

'And Mr Dawes, in the fish shop. He's started speaking Italian. And there's the floating butcher, Miss Darling's giant beanstalk, and your sweets.'

'What about my sweets?'

'Jacob – no one normally has sweets that explode like sparklers in their mouth.'

'Awesome,' says Jacob pulling a paper bag from his pocket and examining the contents. 'And you think it's the dust from the castle? Think of the possibilities – I mean, you could . . .' He waves his arm for inspiration, sending a shower of sparks over Eric's hair.

'Steady on,' says Eric, dousing himself. 'Anyway – it could be really dangerous.'

'Did anyone else have the sense that time stopped?' I say. 'In the town hall, when your dad clambered into the box.'

Jacob sheds a small flame; Eric drips.

'What do you mean?' asks Eric. This time he really is crying.

'I was worried about your dad going into the disappearing cabinet – because it genuinely does disappear things. But I think someone interfered.'

'Who?' asks Eric.

'Lily's dad – I think he has a meteorite. I think he did something while your dad disappeared – I just haven't worked out what it was.'

Chapter 20

'But I don't want chocolate beetroot cake! I want multicoloured rainbow cake!' Tilly snarls in the doorway. 'And no one's given me ANY PRESENTS YET!'

I turn away and stare through the kitchen window into the model village, watching the church grow and shrink like a living being. It might be that dust; there's more of it all the time. This morning I was all sticky with it and couldn't get my socks on properly. We're going to have to do something about it.

We're going to have to do something about Eric's dad too – he still hasn't turned up. And it's been more than twelve hours. Grandma was so sure he would be here somewhere, within the village, but I'm worried that she's wrong. Eric slept with us last night, but rushed back to check the house first thing this morning.

I feel about 75% bad about Eric's dad. I should have stopped him going in the disappearing cabinet – but it's at least 25% my dad's fault, because he's a grown-up and should know better.

And I'm pretty sure it's at least 47% the professor's fault.

'Tilly,' says Grandma. 'I got up at five to make your cake. It's very special and you will like it.'

Personally I wouldn't argue with Grandma, but I hear Tilly's intake of breath as she prepares to let off one of her killer screams, so I make a run for it.

I make it to the garden by the time the scream breaks. It's bad – very bad – but gets worse when the stupid cockatoo, which no one can catch, lands on the growing church tower and joins in with 'Tom made a stinky one', before flying off, laughing.

I hesitate, watching a tall column of grass-green smoke rise from the model blacksmith's forge. I look back towards the house. I wonder if I should hang around to help Grandma, or join Eric looking for his dad. He's searching the model village, on his hands and knees, in case his dad's somehow been shrunk.

While I'm standing in the garden, I see Lily Lee creep towards the house. She looks as if she doesn't want to be seen.

For a moment I wonder whether to keep quiet and just see what she's up to, but then decide that'll only get embarrassing, so I step up to the fence. 'Lily,' I say.

'Oh!' she says, jumping. 'I – um.'

'What are you doing here?' I ask, immediately wishing I'd just hidden in a bush and kept quiet.

'Tilly's birthday,' she says, handing me an envelope. 'Just wanted to give her a card – I can't come to the party.'

I take the card, but notice that in her other hand, she seems to be holding a hammer, even though it's tucked behind her back.

She sees me staring at it.

'Oh – er – thought I'd do a bit of fossil hunting,' she says and walks off down the street.

Chapter 21

Tilly's party has begun. I tried to leave, but Mum asked me to stay and be helpful. When the birthday cake is finally wheeled out into the garden her friends go into peals of squeally delight.

It's pink – of course – layered, like a wedding cake, and if it started off as chocolate beetroot, it now looks more like strawberry. Grandma may have tried to turn it into a rainbow cake, but I can't be sure. Everything's oozing with cream and buttercream and fruit. What might be an icing cockatoo is sliding down the side. It's about a Tilly tall and a Tilly wide – and yes, I was helpful, because without my swift intervention – plunging my hands into the buttercream – the enormous top would have slipped sideways from the enormous bottom as they brought it out. In my view, it's a catastrophe, but the girls and their parents make cooing noises as if it's a masterpiece.

'And now for Tilly's birthday surprise,' says Dad, turning the cake around, and revealing a cardboard box buried deep inside.

I don't watch as Mum and Dad argue with Tilly over the

best way to get into the box. Instead, my attention is caught by the sight of Professor Lee wandering up to our house with a wheelbarrow. He's wearing a dusty, baggy sweater, a baseball cap, shorts and work boots. Almost a disguise.

He walks around to the garage door and prods it. I know it'll just swing open and from there he'll be able to get into the house, so I rush back into the kitchen, through the hall and peek my head around the door that goes into the garage.

I can just see the wheelbarrow wheel under the opening door.

'Well, of course, when we do magic . . .' I say loudly in my deepest Dad voice, crashing the hall door behind me as I go into the garage. The wheelbarrow retreats, and I rush towards the main garage door, slipping the rusty old bolts down until they rest in the concrete floor.

That feels 110% good. Whatever Professor Lee was doing trying to get into our garage – he shouldn't have been.

Standing on tiptoe, peering through the smeary pane of glass in the door, I see the back of his sweater disappear around the corner towards the castle.

'Aaaaaah!!!!' A scream more deadly than Tilly's earlier cake scream burns my eardrums.

I rush back out of the garage, through the hall and the kitchen. From the steps, I see Tilly pinned against the model village fence by an enormous snake, a strawberry balanced on its head.

Behind it are the smashed remnants of the cake, and a trail of cream and sponge leads over the grass to where the snake is now, glaring at Tilly.

Mum and Dad are just standing there with their mouths open, and the other girls have climbed to safety in their parents' arms, so it's just Tilly facing the snake alone.

Tilly's eyes are locked with the snake's. It's hard to see who is more deadly.

'Is it poisonous?' I say quietly, staying absolutely still.

'It is,' whispers Eric, silently appearing beside me, still without his dad. 'It's almost certainly poisonous, it's got a "V" on its head and it's twice the size it ought to be. So there'll be twice as much venom. Could you shrink it?'

I hold up my hand. 'I can't get a clear shot – Tilly would shrink too. How about water?'

'I'd have to move a lot closer to really squirt it,' says Eric.

I'm just trying to work out how I could get a decent shrinking view of the snake, when Tilly springs over the fence. The parents gasp and cheer, but the snake's not stupid and it's not slow – it slides through the fence slats, shedding creamy blobs, and I see its tail vanish at about the same time as Tilly leaps on her bike and begins to pedal.

'Quick, after her!' I shout, running towards the gate.

Eric goes over to inspect the snake's broken box.

'No time for that now!' I say. 'I need you, Eric – we'll have to get Jacob – we've got to save Tilly!'

Chapter 22

We charge down the village street. Eric's panting behind me, Tilly's way ahead – but so's the snake.

'Get Jacob,' I shout, 'and catch me up.'

''K,' pants Eric, crashing to a halt against Jacob's garden fence. I run on, following Tilly's trail. She seems to be heading towards the castle. But that's so stupid. If she gets stuck in those tunnels with the snake she won't stand a chance. For the first time in my life I experience something that might possibly be love for Tilly. Actually, I wouldn't go so far as love – but I am worried about her.

Behind me, I hear Eric and three milk bottles crash out of Jacob's gate and race down the street.

'Jacob gave me this,' shouts Eric. I look back. Eric's holding a Batman walkie-talkie. 'He'll be with us as soon as he's dressed.'

'Dressed?' I call over my shoulder.

But Eric doesn't say anything. All I can hear are his feet thumping on the road.

Way ahead of us, Tilly veers at the last second and plummets into the labyrinth of streets below the castle.

I stop on the castle green, listening for the screams of the tourists when they spot a small girl on a bike pursued by an enormous snake . . . but it's all eerily silent.

'Where have they –' starts Eric, but he's interrupted by Tilly exploding out of an alleyway to our left, pedalling hard back towards the castle, slowed by the long grass of the green.

Eric leaps forward and sprays the grass – and Tilly – with an absurd amount of water.

'Why did you do that?' Tilly screams.

'Mud!' he shouts. 'I don't think snakes do mud.'

As the snake emerges from the alleyway, it slows, eyes the bog that Eric's created, and pauses. 'Brilliant idea,' I shout at Eric. I stand back and make an 'O'.

YES!

Click.

But all I get is a circle of very small, wet grass. No snake.

'Big J, here.' A burst of noise crackles from the walkie-talkie, echoing around the buildings. 'Do you read me? Roger – over and out.'

For a moment, the snake stops, as if it's noticed us for the first time. I try to shrink it again. I end up with another circle of grass. I don't understand; it should have worked.

'We're at the castle green,' Eric hisses into the walkie-talkie, fumbling for the volume button. 'Snake's here, so's Tilly.'

'Yes, and I'm soaking wet, no thanks to you,' Tilly snarls, her eyes fixed on the snake.

Eric brushes a tear from the corner of his eye. 'I was only trying to help,' he says.

'Well, don't,' says Tilly, tugging at her wet T-shirt with one hand, the other gripping the handlebars as if they're going to save her. 'This is my favourite T-shirt and I'd rather be bitten than ruin it. I'm going to make you buy me another. Maybe two.' For a moment, I think about walking away and leaving Tilly and the snake to sort it out between them. They deserve each other.

And then I think about what Grandma would say, and stay put.

Tilly looks up towards the snake's giant head and doesn't notice as the pink cockatoo lands on the back of her bike in a flutter of wings, and contemplates a nearby purple cat.

Eric sends a jet of water towards the snake, but as if it hits an invisible wall, the water stops dead and falls to the ground. The snake doesn't notice.

'Thought as much,' Eric says. 'It's the dust. Just like the tunnel, we couldn't do anything. The snake's coated in it, it's growing because of it, so we can't touch it. The dust is simply stronger than us. We'll have to deal with it as if we haven't got powers.'

I look at the vast golden-green creature poised to strike, only a few feet from my sister. It's getting bigger all the time. It wouldn't even fit in a horsebox now. And its teeth? Long curved knives, dripping venom.

Tilly's bending backwards away from them but they'd easily reach her, easily go right through her arm.

I swallow. 'Any suggestions?'

'A hosepipe?' whispers Eric. 'Or the animal rescue people? They must do this stuff all the time.'

'Really?' I say, thinking about the nice man from the rescue centre and his nice wife, and their nice children, surrounded by puppies and kittens.

'Maybe not,' replies Eric.

I wonder where the nearest samurai sword is. If it comes to it, someone's going to have to behead this monster. I hope it isn't me.

'Ta da!' A sound like a foghorn bounces off the castle walls. The snake's head whips around, and I follow its gaze.

It's almost certainly Jacob – I can tell by the shape – but he's made himself even more enormous. Wearing a large colander on his head, he's added roller skates, four huge scatter cushions strapped around his middle, green-and-red 3D cardboard specs, and what must be his dad's pants and vest, over his mum's red tights. Small glittery squares fall from his legs, and I realise they're sweet wrappers. What was once a plastic sword drips melted from one hand, and in the other, he holds a burned breadboard.

Chapter 23

'Oh dear,' says Eric.

'Here I am. Hell Fire Man – Superhero Extraordinaire – solver of the world's problems, saver of maidens and wusses . . .'

'Jacob – careful, your powers won't –'

'Shhh, Scaredy Cat,' says Jacob. 'I'm going to try charming it.'

Tilly's gazing at him, her jaw hanging low. I signal to her to get away, but she's transfixed by Jacob, or possibly the snake. The cockatoo, giving up on the purple cat, flaps its wings and says, 'Oh, look, it's a toilet!' and flies towards the snake.

The snake ducks and stares at the pink thing hovering over its head. The cockatoo's feathers release a small sparkling cloud over the snake's head, and the snake seems to recoil.

Of course, the cockatoo's pink, because of the dust from the castle.

The snake's big, because of the dust.

Dust. If we can't wash it off we could add more.

It's a long shot, but there's nothing else I can think of.

'Quick!' I yell, scooping up two handfuls of the glittery dust from a nearby bench. I fling them over the snake.

Eric swipes his hand over a postbox and makes a soggy dustball, which explodes over the snake's head.

The snake visibly shrinks but continues to eye the cockatoo. Jacob takes a saucepan from his belt and scrapes up an inch or two of dust.

He advances on the snake, holding the saucepan high. 'Here, snakey snakey.'

'No, don't,' I shout.

The snake stops staring at the cockatoo and gazes at Jacob. Tilly giggles; the snake's eyes dart from Jacob to her.

'Come here, little snakey,' says Jacob, well within striking distance.

'He's either incredibly brave or incredibly stupid,' mutters Eric.

I make one last attempt to shrink the snake. Once again, nothing useful happens.

Jacob flings his dust and his saucepan over the creature, and, as he does so, the snake shoots forward and buries its fangs in Jacob's stomach.

'No!' I shout.

Sheets of flame rocket from Jacob's fingers. They crackle over the snake, leaving it unharmed while Jacob staggers backwards howling. 'I'm bitten – I'm bitten! I'm dead – it got me! I never even had time to write my will.'

'Quick,' says Eric, ignoring Jacob and racing for the snake's head. 'Grab the tail.'

I do. It's dry and heavy and cold – and wriggling.

'Tie a bow!' shouts Eric.

Knot would be nearer the truth. But we tussle and bend and wind until the giant snake looks like it's had an accident with a handbag. Its jaws are still wrapped around Jacob's middle, its fangs deeply embedded in the foam cushions wedged behind his belt. I grip the knot in the middle of the snake – not that it could go anywhere, but it feels like the right thing to do – while Eric unties Jacob's belt and the whole outfit collapses. The snake and the cushions thump onto the ground, leaving Jacob standing naked but for roller skates, Speedos and a girl's spotty red-and-white T-shirt. He's not in the least bothered.

He struts through the wreckage of his costume, pushing out his stomach until the T-shirt threatens to rip.

'All you needed was a superhero. Someone incredibly brave, like me. Just to tell you, Snot Face, superherodom is much more useful than brains. See – I've proved it.'

He turns and skates gently back up the hill.

'Well, that answers it,' says Eric. 'He's incredibly stupid.'

Chapter 24

'He's doing it deliberately,' says Eric under his breath.

'Who? What?' I say. We're lying on the roof of Eric's house, using the telescope and a pair of powerful binoculars to watch the village. I'm watching Tilly. She's got the new, plastic box that the shrunken snake was imprisoned in after the episode at the castle. The snake was still pretty big when we caught it, but once we'd used Grandma's hosepipe to wash off the dust, it began to shrink so that it was an ordinary small-knotted-snake size by the time we saw Mum and Dad.

They gawped and Mum said, 'Don't some funny things happen in this village?'

'Quite extraordinary,' agreed Dad, mopping his brow as if he'd captured the knotted snake himself.

I sometimes wonder if my parents have any idea what's going on.

Dad then hid the snake in the crazy golf hut, so that he could return it to the Animal Rescue Centre tomorrow, but Tilly's like a bloodhound when she's looking for something. It took her ten minutes to find it.

I imagine she also discovered that I've found my meteorite.

I get a curious feeling somewhere between smug and terrified. While Tilly thought she had the meteorite, she probably thought she had the upper hand. Now she knows I've got it back, she might start all over again.

Even the thought makes me feel tired.

'The Professor,' says Eric, eventually. 'He's distracting everyone with the dust so that we can't see what he's really up to.'

'Ah,' I say, not really listening. I'm watching Tilly. With these binoculars I can see her hands really clearly. I'm worried that she's going to open the lid. But there's nothing I can do to protect her from her own stupidity – there isn't time for us to get down the stairs, along the road and into the model village before she opens it.

Sometimes I wish I had a mobile phone.

A flurry of wings, and the cockatoo lands on the chimney pots beside us. 'Boys!' it squawks, before flying off again.

Tilly sinks to the ground next to the model village lake and pokes a stick under the edge of the lid.

'Don't,' I say aloud.

'What?' says Eric, his telescope trained on the castle.

'Look.' I point towards the model village.

'Crumbs,' says Eric.

I hold my breath as Tilly slides the stick along under the lid and begins to lever it up.

'Here it comes,' I say.

The lid pops open and I brace myself, waiting for a super-fast stab from the snake. Nothing happens. Tilly leans forward and peers into the box.

'Don't do that,' says Eric, beside me.

She reaches for her stick and pokes the snake. I hold my breath again. I'm in awe of her lack of imagination. She pulls back on the twig and hoists the tiny, knotted snake from the box. It honestly looks about the size of one of Jacob's rubber worms that he put down Mrs Worthy's back at the first session of Field Craft this summer.

'Whoa,' breathes Eric. 'It's minuscule! It's gone on shrinking.'

'But she can't keep it,' I say. 'It'll grow again.'

For a moment I can't see her as my view is interrupted by a string of white vans whizzing up the road from the castle and on out of the village.

When the vans have gone, and I can see Tilly again, she's dangling the snake in the pond. It can't swim, not least because it's all knotted. 'She's going to drown it! Even for Tilly that's a bit cruel.'

'What's he doing?' Eric points towards the front of our house. Professor Lee's lurking outside our garage again, this time with no wheelbarrow.

'What's she doing?' I point to Lily Lee, standing flat against the wall, further along the street. 'She looks as if she's watching him.'

The professor tries the garage door, glancing around himself and pressing on the most battered panel at the end. He's obviously pushing quite hard because his feet are sliding on the road.

The door gives way and he plunges into the darkness.

'Oh dear,' says Eric.

A second later, the professor appears in the doorway with the huge and heavy disappearing cabinet.

'How's he . . . ?'

The question's answered by another white van racing up from the castle. It screeches to a halt outside our house.

'No!' I shout, but behind the van Grandma bursts out of our front door, her arms full of Eric's dad's clean washing. The van driver panics, and takes off down the road, leaving the professor standing in the garage doorway holding the disappearing cabinet and looking absolutely thunderous.

Grandma doesn't spot him, just carefully locks the front door before heading in our direction.

Chapter 25

We make the landing a millisecond before she knocks on the door. She comes into the kitchen and stares at us.

'You two are up to something,' she says, folding the washing neatly and squeezing it into a bulging chest of drawers that stands in the corner. Eric's house is not normal – no one's clothes are in their bedrooms, and the kitchen things seem to live all over the house. 'I can tell.'

'We were . . .' I say.

'Looking for Dad,' says Eric. Which is partly true. We were looking for Eric's dad although I was mainly spying on Tilly.

'Ah,' says Grandma, peering at the washing. 'Yes – he could be very close, you know . . . Don't give up hope.' She stares into the middle distance and sighs. 'Things do have a tendency to happen to poor Colin.'

A tear trickles down from underneath Eric's glasses. It might just be out-of-control water but he wipes it with his sleeve and sniffs loudly. 'Well, thanks for doing the laundry, Mrs Perks. Shut the door on your way out, I've got a key . . .' He bolts for the door.

I follow, and we race down towards home. We check for the disappearing cabinet, which is still there, slam the garage door shut and make it round to the model village just in time to see Tilly drop the snake back into the box and strut into the house carrying it under her arm.

'So she didn't get bitten?' I say, trying to keep the disappointment out of my voice.

'Obviously not,' says Eric. 'But we can't leave it with her.'

We cram into the house, intercepting Tilly at the bottom of the stairs. She stands with the box in her hands, her bottom lip sticking out. And she breathes deeply like someone about to enter combat.

'Don't take that upstairs. You don't know what might happen,' says Eric.

Tilly doesn't say anything. She lowers her head like a bull, waiting to charge.

'Please, Tilly, give it here.'

'Why, Thomas Perks, do you think you are any safer with this creature than I am?' she says.

'Because – I am,' I say. 'Because I'm going to take it away from the house, and . . .' I look across at Eric.

'And – rehabilitate it,' he says. 'It is all right, isn't it?'

'Sort of,' says Tilly, looking uncomfortable. 'It might . . . not be quite as well as it was.' She puts the box down and opens the lid. 'It sort of might have gone to sleep? Stupid useless creature.'

'Oh,' says Eric, prodding the motionless, knotted snake, now closer to an elastic band than a fearsome predator. 'It might be dead.' We stare in silence. Tilly has quite possibly drowned it.

'In which case,' says Tilly, cheerfully, 'I'm going to ask for another pet. The stupid snake died, and the stupid cockatoo flew away. This time, I'm going to get something worth having.' Abandoning the box, Tilly swings on her heel and marches towards Mum and Dad's room. 'Dad! Mum! I NEED A NEW PET!'

I watch her stamping up the stairs. She seems more obsessed with a new pet than she is with getting me to shrink things. I feel at least 47% better about the Tilly situation. I'd feel 77% better if we could actually get rid of the snake.

We gaze into the box. 'It might be my imagination, but that creature seems to be moving.'

'I don't think it is dead,' whispers Eric. 'Come on – time to deal with it, properly. Let's take it back to the source of the trouble.'

Chapter 26

Eric wants to deliver the snake to Professor Lee. He says it's the professor's fault that it got out of control so he should have to deal with it. But since we captured the snake there earlier, a load of giant trucks have arrived on the castle green – huge lorries covered in chunks of girder and painted boarding and acres of green tarpaulin. Their tyres have cut deep ruts in the grass and a group of men are guiding a lorry loaded with something enormous and pink into an absurdly small space.

'Oh,' says Eric. 'A fairground – here?'

I stand behind him, holding the snake box. 'Does it matter?' I ask.

Ten men and a crane haul a vast piece of scaffolding from the truck and pull it upright. It's the beginnings of a roller coaster, a really tall one; one that would tower over the castle walls.

Eric sighs. 'I don't know,' he shrugs. 'Everything's so out of control already, what difference would an out-of-control fairground make?' He stands on the mud at the side of the green looking desolate and I notice he's dripping. It's as if in all this dust chaos, he's losing control of his power. I imagine he's also starting to miss his dad. Even though my parents are the most awful and embarrassing things on the planet – if they disappeared I'd miss them. If Tilly disappeared, I'd even miss her.

We turn away from the fairground and go up a set of stone steps to the rampart surrounding the inner grassy courtyard of the castle. Sitting on the top step is a bored security guard, texting.

'What?' says the security guard. He doesn't even bother to look up.

'We're looking for Professor Lee,' I say.

The security guard points backwards over his shoulder. 'There,' he says. 'He's in; you can tell by the smoke.'

Over the top of the rampart, and down another flight of steps, a tiny rusty brown caravan sits alone in an island of yellowed grass.

Eric grabs the snake box and strides over as if he's about to knock on the door, but pauses with his hand in the air.

'NOOOOOO!' comes a shout from inside. 'That's far too much of the dust, Dad – you'll blow us up.'

Eric turns to look at me. 'Lily?' he mouths.

'Don't be such a ninny – I didn't get where I am today without a few risks.'

BANG!

Eric leaps back and a trail of dark blue smoke trickles from above the door.

'That was silly,' coughs Lily. 'Dangerous, actually.'

'I wouldn't call it dangerous – more . . . exciting,

thrilling . . . full of potential. I mean, look at that disappearing cabinet – it genuinely works: that daft man Colin Threepwood disappeared!'

Lily coughs.

'What?' says the professor.

'Nothing,' she says. 'Just the smoke.'

'But isn't it marvellous? My name will live for ever in the scientific mining community. Gold, silver and a new precious metal – Lee's Quantonium.' Clinking sounds of glass on glass and a mild hissing sound come from the caravan. 'And, most excitingly, there's still more to discover. We don't know how it's going to react to other things. Think of the possibilities!'

'Think of the consequences,' interrupts Lily. 'Dad – you have no idea what all this dust is unleashing here. Did you see the giant snake?'

'Good, wasn't it?' says the professor with a chuckle.

'It could have killed Tilly Perks.'

'But it didn't . . . now, I wonder how the dust gets on with radiation?'

Eric and I move closer to the window. I can see the ceiling and the far wall. All surprisingly white and high-tech and it must be an illusion, but it looks bigger on the inside than the outside.

'Dad – don't.'

More clinking, more hissing and a flash of intense white light crackles from the caravan windows, followed by another enormous bang.

'Dad – you're going to kill us!' yells Lily.

'Yes!' shouts the professor gleefully. 'Yes – yes – yes! But in the cause of science!'

I'm wondering whether to look closer or run away, when everything goes quiet.

'Dad – look at me!' commands Lily. There's silence, then something glass hits the floor and smashes. Moments later, footsteps sound on the boards of the caravan floor and the latch of the door is pulled back.

'Run,' I hiss at Eric and we throw ourselves over a low wall out of sight. Above us, at the top of the steps, the security guard is still texting, apparently not at all bothered by the explosions behind him.

Peering back over the wall I can see the caravan doorway. Professor Lee is walking down the wooden steps through a cloud of purple smoke, followed closely by Lily. The professor's eyes are curiously blank, as if he's really asleep.

'The tunnel,' says Lily clearly, and the professor turns and crosses the grass towards the entrance to the mine. He pauses.

'Professor Lee,' says Lily's voice, like some distant computer. 'Do as you're told. Walk into the darkness.'

And he does.

Chapter 27

'C'mon,' I say after about ten minutes, and, keeping low to the ground, we scuttle over the gate and towards the entrance of the tunnel. It seems darker than last time.

'Should we follow?'

'Um,' says Eric.

I can hear Lily's voice, but not the words she's saying. I feel we ought to follow, but then again . . . I don't really want to. It's different doing things with Jacob, because he's too stupid to be afraid of anything. Eric's wise, so when he's not sure, I'm not sure.

Something metal clangs, and keys turn in a lock. Then there are more footsteps and I can hear that they're returning along the corridor.

'That's it, walk towards the light,' says Lily. 'Keep going, you'll be fine.'

I dive behind the skip. Eric follows.

'A little further, and we'll stop,' says Lily. 'I'm going to click my fingers. When I do so, you will wake. You will remember the disappearing cabinet, the stage, the lights. You will remember climbing inside it, and the door closing. Then you will recall a period of darkness.' She pauses. 'In your deep thoughts, you will remember that you have been to a strange land with snow and hurricanes, steaming geysers, and chairs on a beach. You will remember scratching the word "hope" on a rock and worrying about how to get home to your son. Is this understood?'

'Yes,' says a voice. 'It is.'

'Dad?' says Eric, standing up. 'Dad – is that you?'

Eric's dad stands there blinking in the light. Lily is behind him, her eyes wide with shock as we run from behind the skip and stop in front of her.

'What's going on?' demands Eric.

But Lily clicks her fingers and vanishes. I don't mean she runs away: she vanishes. One minute she's there, and the next she isn't.

'Eric,' says Eric's dad, rushing forward and clutching his son like a life raft.

'Dad,' squeaks Eric from inside the bear hug. 'I've missed you. Dreadfully.' A small spout of water shoots from his hair over his dad's head and this time I can definitely see tears streaming down his face and under his collar.

'Lily?' I say, looking behind the skip. 'Where did she go?' But Eric and his dad are too thrilled about seeing each other to worry about disappearing girls. They stumble out past the smoking caravan and the security guard to stand at the top of the steps looking down into the castle green. They're holding hands, as if they never want to lose each other again.

There's simply no sign of Lily, so I pick up the snake and follow Eric. Through the white plastic, I can see it moving, slowly, and it's still tiny. And still knotted.

'Eric,' I say, holding up the box. 'What are we doing with this snake? The professor's disappeared, so we can't give it to him. I think Lily took him down the tunnel.'

Eric blinks. 'Something's happened, hasn't it? Look at the shadows. Time's slipped again.'

I look at the pool of shade by the castle. It's in the wrong place for the time of day; it seems to have become an evening shadow though it's only the middle of the afternoon. But then I look down at the fairground. It's almost completely built, which is miraculous as we've only been up here for twenty minutes. Haven't we? I don't have a watch to check, but it feels like only twenty minutes.

'What on earth is going on?' I say.

I'm beginning to think there's only one person who can answer this question, but she's just vanished.

Lily Lee.

Chapter 28

At the fairground entrance we find the Worthys. Mrs Worthy is painting something on a piece of bent cardboard sticky-taped to a plastic mop. Mr Worthy is holding it still.

'Ah – Eric, Tom, Colin – would you like to join our protest?'

I look at the Worthys' half-painted placards. 'No fun here', 'Beware of the grass' and 'Make it Fair for Nature'. And one that says: 'Save Fresh Air and Badges'. I assume she means badgers.

'We can't, we've got to re-home this.' Eric points at the snake. I lift the corner of the lid and Eric's dad and Mr and Mrs Worthy all peer into the box.

'Why's it in a knot?' asks Mrs Worthy.

'Long story,' I say, glancing at Eric.

'Goodness! It's a Venomous Polar Sea Snake – terribly rare,' says Eric's dad. 'I've never seen one in the flesh. Where did you get it?'

'Long story,' says Eric, glancing at me.

'Put it back in the sea, then,' says Mr Worthy. 'Perhaps it can swim home.'

Two men from the fairground walk past; they've got oily hands and oily hair. One of them is carrying a huge spanner. He looks scary.

'Keep off our grass. Up with Nature,' calls Mrs Worthy. 'Please.'

'Yes, please don't damage the wildlife, there are toads here,' says Mr Worthy, faintly. 'Rare ones.'

I look at the ground, wondering just how fast I can run if things turn nasty. Spanner man examines the Worthys' grass placard. He glances up at Mr Worthy, who looks as if he might like to run even faster than me.

Spanner man lets out a long, pained sigh. 'That sticky tape's doing a rubbish job. I've got a staple gun that'll fix that sign. Be back in a mo.' He rests the enormous spanner on his shoulder, and strides off towards a van.

'Gosh – thanks,' says Mr Worthy. 'That'd be nice.'

'Thank you – just remember to walk carefully on the grass while you're getting it,' says Mrs Worthy. 'Please.'

With Eric and his dad, I run for the sea.

We lay the snake on the pebbles and Eric's dad uses an ancient snake-charming technique to pacify it. Between the three of us, and with the help of a damp tissue from Eric's pocket, we manage to unknot it. The snake looks at the land, and then at the water.

'Go on, snake, swim away,' Eric's dad says.

It looks back at us, completely without fear, as if being knotted was a slight inconvenience, lifts its head in the air and plunges into the water, swimming fast and purposefully towards the open sea.

'And don't come back,' I say, remembering its fangs hanging over Tilly.

Eric's dad stares at the water as if he's remembering something himself. 'I'm sure at some point recently I was the Mad Hatter, surfing in toothpaste-blue water.'

'Really, Dad?' says Eric. 'I don't think I remember you being the Mad Hatter, but – I was wondering – what would you like to eat, now you're back? I could cook sausages? Or cheesy baked potatoes? Or a pizza?'

Eric's dad looks up towards the sky. The stars are beginning to show and the music of the funfair grinds into action. 'I feel like I've travelled great distances, visited faraway seashores . . . is that possible, do you suppose?' He turns back towards us; he might almost be in tears. 'Have I really been away somewhere?'

Eric blinks and takes off his glasses. 'I don't know, Dad. I don't know where you've been or where you think you've been.' He rubs his eyes. 'I just thought we could have an evening together, comfort food. You know the kind of thing.'

'A roast, Eric; a roast would be very nice,' his dad says quietly. 'Chicken or lamb, with gravy – lots of gravy.'

I look up at Eric's dad, his glasses reflecting the fairground lights in the oncoming night. A tiny blip whisks across from one lens to the other. A shooting star. For a moment I panic, but I see it plummet into the sea. No one can get anywhere near it. It's not dangerous.

Another whizzes past, landing well inland.

'A meteor shower,' says Eric. 'Hmmm.'

Chapter 29

'BUT I WANT TO GO TO THE FAIR!'

Tilly and Dad are heading down towards the castle green. I leave Eric and his dad holding hands looking at the sea, and slip up through the crazy golf to the main street.

Tilly stamps her feet on the cobbles so that the dust flies up all around her. 'Fifty pence!' she bellows. 'Five pounds, more like, or I'll tell Mum you were mean to me –'

'Oh, Tilly, be reasonable,' says Dad. A couple of tourists stop their evening strolls to stare.

Tilly's enjoying the audience. 'You're the one who's unreasonable.' She pauses and slumps her shoulders, looking pathetic. 'I mean, you're the one who makes me work every scrap of the day cleaning the house –' she wipes her hand across her forehead, tragically – 'sweeping chimneys . . .' She lets out a tiny sob. 'And I'm so sorry I couldn't fix the roof – I'm just too small.'

'Poor child. In this day and age,' says a woman to her husband, casting a glare at Dad.

'Tilly,' I say, catching them up.

'Shuttup, Tom!' she hisses. 'I'm just getting somewhere.'

'I know a secret!' The cockatoo, now tinged with yellow, flies overhead, going into orbit around Dad's head. 'I know a secret! I know a secret! I know a secret about YOU!'

'Wretched bird,' says Dad, flapping his arms.

'Five pounds?' says Tilly.

Dad makes a noise somewhere between a grunt and a squeal. It means he's given in.

'Excellent, so glad you see sense,' says Tilly, dropping the hangdog look. 'I want to go on the helter-skelter, with the princess pamper party.' Tilly points at a monstrous pink tower, which is vying with the jaws-of-death underwater upside-down roller coaster for the most-ridiculous-thing-in-the-fairground prize.

'Can't you make do with a ride on the teacups?' says Dad, looking green.

The woman and her husband look confused and wander off up the road.

'You shouldn't give in to her, Dad,' I say, walking into the fairground behind them. 'She'll get worse.'

Dad hands Tilly two pounds and she rushes off to the Princess Pamper Helter-Skelter. 'I don't know how to get out of it – she's so . . . she's so . . .'

'Manipulative?' I say.

We watch Tilly take a pink mat and settle herself at the top of the slide. She waves and sets off, sliding into the pampering zone halfway down.

'Fail, fail, epic fail!' yells the cockatoo from the top of the helter-skelter.

We wait, watching the slide for another view of Tilly. 'Yes, that's probably the right word,' says Dad. 'I can't imagine where she gets it fr—'

Something loud and fast crashes in through the air – a flash of light – heading straight for the helter-skelter; heading straight for the pamper zone.

Bang!

The cockatoo takes off, squawking, and Dad runs towards the helter-skelter. I stand there gawping. I really hope what I think has happened, hasn't happened.

'Dad – Tom!' yells Tilly, running out from the bottom of the tower, shedding marshmallows and cake from a huge pink bag and holding something in her hands.

'Look what I've got! Look what I've got! My very own meteorite!'

Chapter 30

'That's nice, dear,' says Dad, taking the meteorite from Tilly's hand. 'I don't expect it's really a meteorite. Probably a bit of building rubble from the work going on at the castle.'

'It's not, Dad – I know it's –' I kick Tilly and she glares at me. I don't want her to tell Dad about the magic; it would be far too complicated to explain. I'm hoping he and Mum will never have to know.

'What was that mega noise?' It's Jacob, I can tell by the heat. He stands behind me, plunging his hands in and out of a giant bag of jelly shoes. A lace dangles from the corner of his mouth, and lizardlike he sucks it back in.

Tilly stares in disgust, turns to Dad and says: 'Great – now, home, Dad. And – another pet? You promised me another pet.'

For a second Dad creates the illusion that he's in control, and then he droops – I can see he's about to give in. 'Oh no, Tilly, we've done with pets, haven't we? There's been the blasted cockatoo, the savage hamster . . .'

'The snake,' says Tilly, taking Dad by the arm. 'Don't forget the snake.' She leads Dad towards the fairground exit and just as they blend into the crowd, she turns, grins and waves the meteorite at me – as if I'd forgotten.

Jacob's furious that he missed the excitement.

'What? You mean Eric's dad came out of the tunnel?'

I nod, wondering just how Jacob can eat a whole lemon-flavoured trainer without being sick.

'So where was he? Mars? New Zealand?'

I think about it. 'I don't suppose he'd been anywhere,' I say. 'I'm beginning to think that someone around here's messing about with our heads.'

'I knew it,' says Jacob. 'It's the professor. He's an evil genius.' He rootles around in his sweet bag.

'Somehow I don't think it's him.'

'Well, I do,' says Jacob, biting into a lime-coloured sandal. 'Who else could it be?'

I spend the whole night trying to make sense of it all, but I can't.

I toss and turn and stare out of my window at the moon. I'm worried. So far, and it's only been a few hours, Tilly doesn't seem to be able to do anything special. But it's only a matter of time before she learns to become invisible or a magnet or something wildly irritating. I know it's going to happen, and I know it's going to be bad.

Why did she of all people have to catch the blasted meteorite? If Dad had found it, he'd have put it in the rockery or something harmless. But Tilly?

And then there are the Lees. When I put together the facts I know, they just form a random pattern rather like

Grandma's knitting. They obviously want the disappearing cabinet – they've both sniffed around it – but they don't come to get it together. Then there's all the dust and rock that's been mined from the castle, which is Professor Lee, undoubtedly. And I was convinced the professor had a meteorite, I saw it in his hand, but perhaps it wasn't his. Perhaps it wasn't a meteorite at all.

I turn over and gaze at the ceiling. It's still got eight holes in the plaster.

Lily Lee fascinates me. She is a girl, but she's not like the girls round here. She's not at all like Tilly and her friends. I'd really like to have a chat with her, but she keeps on running away. Why did she tell Eric's dad all that stuff about hope and chairs on a beach? And why was he down the tunnel?

And why did she take her dad down the tunnel?

And how did she disappear like that?

I follow the moon shadow across the ceiling until dawn begins to break, and everything outside turns grainy and grey.

That's when I finally fall asleep.

Tilly's vile at breakfast. She sits making smug faces at me over the cornflakes, turning her meteorite over in her hand. Every time Grandma comes past she hides it under the table as if Grandma doesn't know. But Grandma's completely aware of the shooting star last night. I don't think they ever pass over the town without her noticing. And she's completely aware that Tilly's the new owner of a piece of space rock.

But she's taking it very calmly.

Grandma goes into the garage with a bucket of soapy water, looking determined, while I follow Tilly from a distance. Tilly plays with the Woodland Friends. She paints a picture, she wipes her painty fingers on my dressing gown, she stabs compass-point holes in my diary, she eats a peach and leaves the peach stone on my bedside table in a small pool of sticky juice. She does nothing to suggest that she might have powers at all.

At lunchtime, she drags Mum to the Animal Rescue Centre, but they come back empty-handed. 'There was nothing suitable,' says Mum.

'There was a bearded dragon,' says Tilly.

'Don't be silly, Tilly,' says Dad.

'And a really cute hedgehog,' says Tilly.

Mum sighs. 'Covered in fleas.'

'There was that lonely puppy,' says Tilly.

'No dogs,' says Dad.

'A lovely puppy,' says Tilly.

'No dogs,' says Mum.

Tilly growls, and picks up and drops Mum's blue jacket. The dropping looks deliberate. I watch the jacket carefully. It slides to the floor and I notice that the blue is tinged with pink, and glittery – and is it slightly bigger?

Tilly stamps up the stairs. She glances back at the crumpled jacket, a flicker of satisfaction passing over her mouth. So she knows what she can do. I can shrink things, and she can make them larger. But at least when I shrink things they look the same as they did before, only tiny. When she touches something, it's not only bigger, but it bears more than a passing resemblance to the pink, sparkly pamper palace tower from the funfair.

Oh dear.

Chapter 31

'He's down there. You said she put him there – it's the perfect opportunity to get him to confess.' Jacob scorches a casual circle in the grass and points towards the tunnel before clapping his hand over his mouth. 'Ow,' he says. 'I forgot.'

We're standing by the deserted caravan, above the fairground. It hasn't got going for the day yet; instead of people, it's populated by desolate plastic bags blowing through the rides and sticking to abandoned toffee apples.

'She did,' says Eric, cautiously. 'But don't forget, our powers don't work down there.' Below us, Mr and Mrs Worthy emerge from behind the roller coaster, collecting up the rubbish and making sounds of disapproval.

'I vote we should go and find him down the tunnel. I'll go first.' Jacob strides over the grass to the tunnel entrance and stops, staring into the depths. This time, there don't seem to be so many lights. Actually, there don't seem to be any lights.

For a moment, Jacob looks almost doubtful. He sets fire to a paper bag wafting over the courtyard, and we watch as the grey skeleton of the paper floats up and off.

'Should we . . . ?' starts Eric.

'Come on, scaredy cats,' interrupts Jacob, as he marches into the darkness.

I hear Eric suck in some air as he follows me in.

Tunnels are really weird in the dark, especially glittery ones. Every now and again a puff of coloured light illuminates the tunnel for a second. I get a silhouetted glimpse of Jacob's back and then it all goes dark again.

'What's that light?' whispers Jacob.

'Last time we had the flying red glowing things,' says Eric. 'Maybe it's the same.'

The sound of loud scratching fills the darkness.

'A rat?' says Eric.

I don't much like the idea of rats in a dark tunnel and stop, letting Eric go in front of me.

'HELP!' comes a yell from in front of us.

'Who's that?' says Jacob.

'HELP ME! I've been imprisoned.'

We follow the voice until we reach the door to the first of the little caves off the side of the tunnel. The one full of coloured plastic tubs.

'Hello!' I call.

'Oh heavens, is that help I hear?' comes a voice from inside.

'Professor?' I ask.

'Yes, yes, it's me – I don't understand what happened, I'm trapped.'

I run my hands over the wooden door. I can't actually

feel a lock.

'I'll burn it down,' says Jacob. 'Stand back.'

'Wait!' cries Eric, his hands thumping into the door. 'Do we want to release him? I mean, this is in some ways perfect: he's safely locked away, he can't do whatever it is he is doing.'

'What is he doing? We should ask,' I say.

'What are you doing?' yells Jacob at the door. 'With the mining and everything. Until you tell us, we won't let you out.' Jacob turns to us. 'Right sort of thing?'

We stand waiting and listening. There's more scratching but no more puffs of coloured light.

'Professor? We're serious,' I say.

'Boys, boys – I'm not doing anything. I'm just a scientist, testing the rock.'

'Testing four van loads a day?' says Eric. 'I wouldn't think you'd need that much – and it must have cost a fortune to dig this tunnel. We're not idiots, you know; we know there must be some money in it.'

'No – we're not idiots,' echoes Jacob.

'I'm finding things out for the wider world,' says the professor, accompanied by the clink of glass.

'Well – what is going on?' asks Eric.

'I'm just doing some prospecting,' says the professor. He's further away from the door now.

'You're stealing the rock, you mean.'

'I wouldn't go that far. I'm testing it, in my London laboratory – I'm sure it has some very unusual properties.' Something clinks and something rustles against the other side of the door. 'Anyway, now that you know I'm just an ordinary scientist, who has made an extraordinary discovery, are you going to let me out?'

'I think we should find the police,' says Eric.

'Ah –' says the professor. 'In that case . . .'

I lean towards the door to listen.

BANG!

Something throws me across the tunnel. My head cracks on the side and I feel darkness wash over my head like deep, black water. As I fall into the depths, I hear the professor's laugh – a wild, scary sound – and he says something – it sounds like 'Suckers!' My mind tries to make sense of it, but it might as well be coming through soup.

Chapter 32

Eric was completely right. Nothing works here. Or at least, nothing works properly. When my head clears, Jacob and Eric are waving their arms around, attempting to get their powers going next to a metal gate that I'd never noticed before, halfway up the tunnel. Beyond it there's light.

'Let me have another go,' yells Jacob, sending a limp stream of sparks from his fingertips.

'Honestly, the rock's too powerful,' says Eric. 'You won't get anywhere. It's hopeless.'

'Tom,' shouts Jacob. 'Come here and do something useful.'

My head still reeling from the explosion, I stagger over to them and stare at the problem. It's an enormous, very solid padlock. I put my finger and thumb together to form an 'O', and concentrate.

Click.

Absolutely nothing happens.

I try again.

Click.

The lock might possibly be marginally smaller – but I doubt it. 'We're stuck,' I announce and sink back against the wall. 'He's locked us in.'

'Pleased to see the boy genius has grasped the situation,' says Jacob.

'He made a smoke bomb,' says Eric. 'I couldn't see a thing. Couldn't breathe either. By the time I worked out which way was up, he'd gone.'

Jacob goes quiet and draws a circle on the ground with his finger. A single weak spark rises and dies. 'I was . . . confused by the bang,' he says. 'I couldn't – stop him.' He sounds disappointed in himself.

'None of us could,' says Eric in consolation. 'We didn't stand a chance.'

'Yeah . . . but . . .' says Jacob, shrugging and stuffing his hand in his pocket for a shoelace sweet to suck. All his confidence seems to have evaporated. I suspect that he's only eating to make himself feel better – he surely can't be hungry again.

I run my fingers over the barred gate. We're quite a way down the tunnel, and no one outside knows we're here. Inside, it's silent – the mine must be deserted. If we can't find a way out, then we could languish for days on a diet of jelly shoes, until we die of sugar overload or starvation. Whichever happens first.

I imagine Mum and Dad wandering the streets and the beaches searching for us. Grandma keeping up a lonely vigil at the front door, waiting for us to come home. And us dying, one by one, Eric first, because he's the skinniest, Jacob last, days after me. Perhaps I should keep a diary, so that they can read it when they find our skeletons.

I wipe the dust from my hands onto my shirt.

Dust again. And here there's so much. The professor managed to cause an explosion with it – enough to get out of the door. But we wouldn't know how to do that, unless . . .

'Jacob, can you make a spark?'

A tiny light flickers and dies at the end of Jacob's finger. 'Not much of one,' he says.

'That's useless,' says Eric. 'Rubbish.'

I look at Eric. He's never normally unkind.

'Try again, Jacob,' I say.

Jacob grunts and sends a larger spark over the dust. It lasts almost a second before it dies.

'Pants!' says Eric. 'That was pants.'

'Shut up, Snot Face,' says Jacob. 'I'd like to see you do it.'

'I bet I could do better – if I had your power. You're useless.'

Jacob's eyes glow red for a millisecond. I think I can see what Eric's doing. I take my shirt off and lay it on the ground behind the gate.

'Bet you can't set my shirt on fire,' I say.

'Bet I can,' Jacob replies and a sheet of flame leaps out and incinerates the shirt before I can even step back.

'Ow!' howls Jacob, clutching his mouth. Even in the darkness of the tunnel I can see the steam rising from his tongue. It must hurt but we have to keep trying if we're going to get out of here.

'Quick,' I shout. 'More clothes – put them on the fire.'

Eric strips off his lumpy hand-knitted sweater.

'What are we doing?' asks Jacob, staring.

'We don't know how to make an explosion, but we can make smoke,' I yell. 'We need smoke, lots of it.'

Jacob runs back down the corridor and appears with some ragged planks ripped from the prison door. 'Great!' he yells, tearing off his T-shirt and chucking it onto the fire too.

'Signals,' says Eric. 'We could make smoke signals. Mr and Mrs Worthy'll spot them. They're just out there, picking up rubbish – they'll be able to get us out. Right – how do you spell SOS in smoke?'

Chapter 33

The fire burns for about an hour and Eric flaps a piece of cardboard over it, creating intermittent smoke signals. Eventually, having burned the cardboard, we resort to dust to try and keep the flames going, at which point the smoke turns purple and glittery and quite a lot of it refuses to leave the tunnel.

'Well, that was clever, Model Village,' splutters Jacob. 'Now we've got no clothes, and we're still stuck in the tunnel, and we've been gassed by magic smoke. Fan-tas-tic. How I love to see an idiot realise his full potential.'

'It was worth a try,' says Eric sadly.

I feel about 1% good.

It's no good having superpowers, if your superpowers don't work.

I sink back against the wall and bury my head in my hands. I go back to the skeleton diary thoughts again, and wonder if there's some paper down the tunnel somewhere.

'So what did you wish for – Snot Face?' asks Jacob, stretching a jelly lace to see just how far it will go.

'You know wishes don't work if you tell anyone.

Anyway – perhaps I didn't wish.'

'Bet you wished for extra maths homework,' says Jacob.

'Don't be silly, Jacob,' I say.

'What did you wish for?' asks Eric.

'Well, I didn't wish for world peace,' says Jacob, turning to scratch something onto the tunnel wall with his belt buckle.

I glance at Eric. He drops his eyes, and I notice that every visible scrap of his face turns a deep crimson.

So he did wish for world peace.

World peace would be nice. I can see how he might have chosen it. Perhaps, given the power of the meteorites, it's even possible. Perhaps when Eric grows up he'll become an international diplomat, a watery one. Perhaps, even now, he can solve some of the world's problems – on a small scale.

Jacob's managed to carve 'Gerls R wet' into the tunnel wall.

'Hello?' A voice comes through the smoke, followed by coughing.

'Hello?' says Eric. 'Who's there?'

'Us.'

We gaze up into the light as two black silhouettes appear. One's taller, one's smaller; the small one's awfully familiar. 'Tilly?'

'Is that Tom?' Tilly's voice sounds loud.

'Yes – have you got Lily with you?'

'She totally has,' says Lily. 'Oh, and well done for the smoke signals. The Worthys saw them and came to watch them from the model village. They were terribly impressed.

They didn't know where they were from, but when I saw the colour, and the glitter, I was pretty sure.'

'But – it was your dad –' starts Eric.

'Yes,' I say. 'Professor Lee . . .'

'Shhhh! What's that sound?' says Lily, holding up her hand.

Not far away there's a rumble like something massive rolling over the ground.

'It sounds like an enormous truck,' says Jacob. 'From the fairground, perhaps? Are you going to let us out? I'm dying for a drink.'

'It sounds closer than the fairground,' I say.

'I'll go and see,' says Lily, running back up towards the entrance.

'But –' says Eric, 'if you're going to let us out – I don't understand – whose side –'

'No time for explanations,' she interrupts. 'Tilly, you'd better come too.'

'Why?' asks Tilly, still standing by the bars. I can't help feeling she's enjoying the sight of us imprisoned and helpless.

'Revenge?' says Lily.

'Oh, yeah,' says Tilly, turning and running to follow Lily. 'You are so going to owe me after this, Tom Perks.'

'After what?' I call.

But Tilly doesn't answer, she just runs up the tunnel.

'Revenge?' says Eric. 'What?'

'Revenge? On us?' asks Jacob. 'But we haven't done anything.'

We stand by the bars, listening. All I can hear is the crunch of feet on the gritty dust. Then there's the sound of a chain clanking, and a sort of squeaking, simpering sound.

'They've abandoned us,' says Jacob, sliding back onto the ground. 'I knew we couldn't trust them – it's obvious.'

'Shhh,' I say, watching the top of the tunnel. Up near the entrance it all goes black and there's only the faintest grey light that reflects from the walls.

'What's going on?' says Jacob.

'It sounds . . . enormous,' whispers Eric.

He's right. Something huge is snuffling towards us, sniffing and licking and panting. Someone shines a torch at the ceiling, so that the glow falls on the creature heading our way.

It's an enormous pink, glittery thing. It might be a puppy. Its vast head fills the passage; its ears brush the ceiling and walls; its huge tongue trails along the floor.

'Meet Revenge,' says Tilly. 'He's going to rescue you.'

Chapter 34

It stops at the bars. Tilly is almost invisible nestled inside the long pink hairs of its neck ruff, and laughs as it sticks a monstrous tongue through the bars, laden with spit. The tongue waves in the air and we all recoil, although Eric isn't fast enough, his hair going from an orange Afro to a damp jellyfish in seconds.

'Ugh!'

'He's a black Lab,' says Tilly, happily shaking the giant puppy's drool from her hair and persuading the creature to grab the gate in its vast jaws and drop it at the side of the tunnel.

'Looks pink to me,' says Jacob. 'And glittery.' He pushes his way past Tilly, avoiding the puppy's mouth.

'Yes,' says Tilly, doubtfully. 'I don't understand that bit. I seem to be able to make things grow, but they don't just get bigger. It's kind of nice, but –'

'Just try not to touch anything,' I say, rubbing the lump on my head.

A smile flickers over Tilly's lips. 'Hmmm . . .' she says.

'No – don't be tempted,' says Eric. 'Think of the trouble

we had with him when he was tiny.' He nods towards Jacob. 'He's still not right. I don't think you'd actually want your brother to be giant and pink for ever.'

'But it fades,' says Tilly, pushing the puppy's enormous tongue out of her hair. 'Look at Jupiter – it grew back.'

I help Eric past the puppy's vast tail. 'It doesn't always grow back.'

'I think you have to be careful,' says Jacob.

We all stare at him.

'Well, you do. I mean, with my powers I could set fire to something really precious.'

'What? Like your mum?' says Eric.

'No – something more precious than that . . . something like my Game Cube.'

'But you did,' I say. 'At Field Craft.'

Jacob's brow furrows. 'Oh, yeah,' he says. 'Anyway, if it doesn't grow back or whatever, something else nasty might happen. My power makes my mouth burn – it's horrible. I can't eat chilli any more.'

'All powers come with a downside,' says Eric, quietly.

I look across at him, giving him the chance to tell me.

But Jacob wades in. 'Crying,' he says. 'Haven't you noticed? Snot Face can't stop crying. Turned into a right wuss.'

Eric sighs, and Lily appears at the end of the tunnel. 'He's getting away. Quick, everybody, we've got to catch him!'

'Who? What?' asks Jacob.

We don't bother to answer, just race past him into the light.

Tilly's pretty good at riding the puppy. And the puppy's pretty good at running but, like puppies do, it doesn't run in a straight line, so while we pile up the road from the castle, Tilly canters all around the town and back to us again yelping and laughing.

It's like we're a real team of superheroes. Not quite like the ones from the comics – more Bywater-by-Sea than New York – but we are chasing an evil genius, after all, and no one else is going to stop him. The safety of the nation lies in our hands, although I think superheroes are supposed to be fitter and faster than us.

Lily's at the front, Eric and Jacob are at the back. I'm struggling to keep ahead of them.

'He's driving a steamroller,' she stutters. 'He took it from the fair. It's slow but it's impossible to stop.'

'But he's your dad!' pants Eric, trying desperately to keep up. 'Why aren't you helping him?'

Lily doesn't say anything until we pass the model village.

'Because he's wrong,' she says. 'He's never had anything as powerful as the dust that comes out of the castle; he's drunk on the idea of it. He seems to think he can make his fortune and change the world. But he's wrong and that dust's dangerous – you two know that. Remember the snake?'

'Certainly do,' says Jacob, 'I gave him what for!'

'You got bitten,' says Tilly.

'You got wet,' says Jacob. 'And we had to save you.'

'I could easily have got away from him,' says Tilly.

'Why didn't you, then?' I ask.

Tilly sticks her tongue out and leans forward into

Revenge's fur.

'Anyway – why should we trust you?' I ask Lily. 'How do we know you're not going to lead us into some cave and shut us in for a week, like you did to Eric's dad?'

'What!' She stops. 'I thought I'd made you forget.'

'Time did something funny that afternoon, but I didn't forget – did you?' I say to Eric stumbling to a halt beside her.

Eric shakes his head and slumps forward, gasping for breath. 'Probably because we were right next to the castle, covered in dust – powers short-circuited.'

'I hid him,' says Lily. 'I hypnotised the whole audience and took him away. I knew the disappearing cabinet would really work, and I was worried it would send someone somewhere mad like another planet, so I stole your dad and hid him. I hope that was all right – I thought it was for the best.'

Eric's far too nice to be cross with her, but I spot a flicker of irritation cross his lips, and he coughs into his hand to cover it.

'You can hypnotise people?' says Jacob, throwing himself on the ground beside us and panting.

'And animals, although I'm not sure Revenge is really in my power,' says Lily, pointing at the puppy now sniffing around a lamp post. 'I caught a meteorite, when we first arrived. Only it took me a little while to work out what it did.'

'That must have been the one we saw land at the same time as yours,' I say to Jacob and Eric.

'Respect,' says Jacob.

'Wow!' says Eric. 'So you've got a power too?'

'We're a team, we're magical – we can save the world – we can do anything!' shouts Jacob.

For once, I agree with him.

'Yes,' says Lily. 'But if we don't hurry up, even with all the powers we have between us, we won't be able to stop Dad. He'll have got away with it.'

Chapter 35

I don't think the professor can have had steamroller lessons because he manages to take out all the lamp posts, plunging the town into near darkness as he goes. It doesn't slow him down, though, and no matter how hard we run I don't think we can catch up with him. We race through the bungalows at the edge of town, until we pass between the ancient black boundary stones and are past the sign that says '*Thank you for driving carefully through Bywater-by-Sea*'.

'Tom. Shrink him,' yells Eric. 'There's nothing else for it.'

'But Grandma'll kill me,' I say.

'She'll have to kill you, then,' he says. 'Do it.'

So I stop at the side of the road and although it's dark I can see the smoke from the chimney of the steamroller and a few sparks.

I put my thumb and finger together to make an 'O'.

Click.

But when I look up, the steamroller's still there, still chugging away from us.

'Eric,' I cry. 'He must be too far away from me, I can't shrink him!'

'What?' Eric stops. He raises his hand and where a torrent of water should be, nothing happens.

'Jacob,' shouts Lily. 'Try and firebomb him.'

'Really?' says Jacob. 'Your own dad?'

'Yes – really,' she says. 'Go on.'

Jacob raises his shoulders and points his finger in the direction of the steamroller. 'Go, flames, go – do your worst.'

But nothing happens. Not even the tiniest spark.

'Tilly? Can you help?' I shout through the darkness and then I realise that the tiny black thing scuttling around my feet is what used to be the giant pink puppy.

'He shrank,' she says from right next to me. 'He's gone all small and cute.'

'I don't understand,' says Jacob. 'Why can't we do anything?'

'Must be a glitch of some sort,' says Eric, waving his arms at the signpost.

We stand panting, watching the steamroller grind out of sight. I listen for the last hum of the engine. When it's gone, I'll know that we've lost – that the professor will get to London, with the secret of the castle at his fingertips. He'll sell the rock, the dust, make his fortune and ultimately destroy the village.

I droop, wishing that at least one of us had been given the power of flight or that I'd had the intelligence to grab a bicycle on the way past the house.

But the engine doesn't die away completely. It gets louder, and within seconds we see the steamroller thundering back towards us, rumbling down the middle of the road and showing no sign of stopping.

'Jump!' I yell. I throw myself in the ditch, poking my head up over the side to watch it pass, but when it's level with the sign to the town, the thundering steamroller falls to murmuring and finally stops.

The professor climbs down from the seat. He looks exhausted. Defeated.

We walk towards him. Tilly's puppy tugs gently at his trouser leg.

The professor turns to Lily. 'It doesn't work.'

'What do you mean, it doesn't work?'

'Watch.' He reaches into his pocket for a small rock and a grater. Carefully, he begins to grate the stone. A steady confetti of dust falls. He walks back and forth past the boundary stones. I notice that when he's on the village side, the dust glitters and sparkles; the grass turns purple, grows and dies all in a second. Outside the village, the dust falls as . . . dust.

Nothing happens.

I hold my finger and thumb together to make an 'O' and try to shrink a boulder lying on the road outside the village boundary.

Click.

Nothing happens. I try the same thing inside the village boundary and the boulder turns to a pebble in my hand.

I look up at the professor. 'You're saying it only works within the boundaries of Bywater-by-Sea. That any of it only works in Bywater-by-Sea. Us – the rock, the meteorites. All of it?'

He nods, unable to speak. From his pocket he takes a matchbox. He strikes a match and holds it against the dust lying on the road. It burns, letting off a golden sparkling smoke, very much like a roman candle firework, and sizzles across the ground, but not a single inch outside the boundary of the village.

He looks up at me. 'It only works in the blasted village. It's useless outside, utterly useless.'

Epilogue

We're on the very last camp-out of the summer.

The grass hasn't quite grown back over the original campfire, so Mr Worthy suggested that we make it on the same spot, only this time Tilly and Jacob are building it together.

Lily Lee's here. She decided to stay in the village until the end of the holidays, lodging with Eric and his dad. Now Eric's using the telescope to teach her how to spot the Crab Nebula, in exchange for which she's shown him the solution to some particularly tedious mathematical equation.

I wonder if she wished for a geeky friend. She's certainly found one, although I'd quite like him back when she's gone.

I'm sticking marshmallows on sticks with Mrs Worthy and six Hedgelings. She's brought some unbreakable biscuits that might or might not be gingerbread men. I think they're probably made of the castle dust, only without the magic.

We've spent the last week cleaning up the dust under Grandma's direction and flushing it all into the sea. I only hope the village doesn't disappear under a troop of giant jellyfish or worse, but on land, things are finally getting back to normal.

Just to test it, Jacob bought a bag of sweets. They were deliciously ordinary.

'Great – super, right, ready for a sing-song?' Mr Worthy crashes onto the grass beside us and strikes up a tune on his guitar.

I think the noise he's making is a tune, it's just it's not any tune I've ever heard before. Mrs Worthy nods her head a little out of time and joins in with some atonal humming.

Two of the Hedgelings find something more interesting to do and I suddenly remember that I could be cooking.

I slip away from the sing-song, open a packet of strange pale vegetarian sausages and lay them in a frying pan. They might as well be made of plastic, and remain utterly silent when I place the pan over a tiny gas cooker.

I watch the little blue flame flickering against the bottom of the pan. It looks so feeble, and somehow it reflects my mood. I can't help feeling a little gloomy. I know I ought to be really pleased that the professor failed, that his plan to sell the rock from under the castle crashed and burned, but deep inside I'm a little disappointed. Partly because, although we have powers, we're not really superheroes, we're just domestic superheroes, but also because just for a moment, I'd thought that Eric's wish might come true. That Bywater-by-Sea might just have been able to achieve world peace, that somehow, between us all, like a real team, we could have done something truly meaningful.

Fat chance.

'I know a secret! I know a secret.' The cockatoo lands in a tree. It turns itself around and shakes the last of the dust from its wings. It's almost completely white now.

'That bird's so funny,' says Mr Worthy, putting down the guitar and moving towards the cockatoo. The bird takes off and lands in a different tree.

'World peace!' it yells over the campsite. 'World peace, world peace!'

'Oh – what a wag!' says Mrs Worthy.

'Almost as if it knew what it was saying,' says Mr Worthy.

I scowl at the cockatoo, and it takes off, circles around our heads, squawks 'goodbye' and flies out to sea.

'Goodbye, bird,' I say, watching it vanish into the darkness.

'Isn't it wonderful,' says Mrs Worthy to Mr Worthy. I look up from the frying pan to see what they mean. Mrs Worthy nods towards Jacob and Tilly.

'No – Jacob,' says Tilly. 'Don't snatch, say please.'

Jacob lets a small puff of steam out of his ears. 'Please, Tilly, may I have the matches?'

'Of course,' says Tilly, sitting back with only a slight suggestion of smugness. 'And later on, I'll show you how to make an internet connection out of macaroni.'

'Yeah, I'd like to know how to do that,' says Jacob, without the faintest hint of sarcasm.

'And those two,' says Mr Worthy, indicating Eric and Lily who are taking it in turns to look through the telescope.

'All because of your efforts, Simon,' says Mrs Worthy, patting her husband on the back.

'And yours, Janey,' says Mr Worthy, strumming a

chord. 'Amazing what a bit of gender equality can do. An unqualified success.'

'Shall we toast with some cocoa?' asks Mrs Worthy, her eyes wide with excitement.

'We could add sugar,' giggles Mr Worthy.

I look up at Eric. He's heard the conversation. He raises his eyebrows in the direction of Tilly and Jacob and smiles.

I nod.

It is remarkable. No one's shouted at anyone else, no one's sabotaged anyone's sleeping bag. Everyone's being civil. Everyone's happy.

I don't for one minute think it's because of the Worthys. Possibly in spite of the Worthys.

But it is remarkable.

And in its way, it's a sort of world peace.

Acknowledgements

Many thanks to all the enthusiastic teachers, librarians and parents who helped make this project happen, to Sara O'Connor for thinking of it, and to the team at Hot Key Books who worked so hard to make it a success, especially Cait Davies (and her mum), Jenny Jacoby, Becca Langton, Amy Orringer, and all those people who pored over the weekly roundups. You know who you are.

Thank you to the Story Adventurers!

The Star List

10SGMF7890
1Dloverxxx
Amber Naeem
Becky Gillan
Belmontwriters
Bunny1 (Teenyweeny HC)
CheekyMonkeyBird
ChoccyWillow
Chocolatelover6 (Teenyweeny JG)
Cupcake11
Cute Skeleton <3
Doughnut123
GorgeousStoryGirl
Hellopeeps
HHstarz
Horses!
Ilovegreyhounds56
Isapop
Izthewiz (Teenyweeny IL)
jamesbond (Teenyweeny EBP)
Jasmine Hale
Jedi 1
Library Club

Liv Booton
London 2012
Love Labradors!
Mario Kart (Teenyweeny JW)
Miss Awesomeness 123
MJS Yr4 Reading Club
No1 girl (Teenyweeny SH)
OneDirection999 (Teenyweeny EJ)
Planet girl (Teenyweeny RR)
Poppet (Teenyweeny KNM)
Glamarous Girl (Teenyweeny RH)
RockyBP
Rosepetals
Ruby Hurford
RVProx
Shakira Saleem
Shivani Sharma
Silveryowl
SpaceRaider (Teenyweeny JS)
Spiderman (Teenyweeny KM)
Spongey900 (Teenyweeny AO)
SweetCandy
SweetChoc
Tails (Teenyweeny CC)
Thea Ralph
Theheart (Teenyweeny HH)
The Rock (Teenyweeny SW)
Year 5, St Clements CE Primary School
Year 6 Book Club

And an extra-special thank you to everyone who pre-ordered this book

Amber Naeem
Amy Coyne
Arwa Saifee Mullamitha
Bay Gorrod
Becky
Dane Baird
Erin Tosh
GSAL Library Club
Hannah Ahmed
Isabella Morgan
Ixworth Middle School Year 6 Book Club
Jamie Whitworth
Liv Booton
Preet Moonga
RosePetals
Sanam Blakesley
Solomon & Rufus Finn
St Clement's CE Primary School
Sydney Williams-Howe
Target Breakers St Josephs Port Talbot
Thea Ralph
Tina Brown

Contributors

1DLoverxxx, 10SGMF7890, 3L, 6Mcrazeballs, alminie gritling, appl353, Arceus, archawesome, Beany, belmontwriters, belmontwriters (C), bluepanda, BookLover04, Books and Writing = me, booney9654, Booty, Booty (Little Boot), Bubble, Bunny1 (Teenyweeny HC), bunnybubbles871, candy, catgirl, Chancelowls, CheekyMonkeyBird, Cheesy, Chicken, ChoccyWillow, chocolate, Chocolatelover6 (Teenyweeeny JG), cookie dough, cookiemonster, Crepsley8, cupcake11, cupcake12, cupcakesweetiepie11, Cuteskeleton <3, cutie pie, DGFU, Diamond123, dogzombies, dolphin11, DonatellaVer$ace, doughnut1234, Dr.Sheep, Electricwombat, Elephant33, Flash, fluffernutter123, Fluffy, fluffyunicorn123, Fudge, Glamarous girl (Teenyweeny RH), googlemonster1234, GorgeousStoryGirl, grapefruit, guy12225, Hellopeeps, Hellopeeps (Amazing Hornets), Hellopeeps (Amazing Hornets 2), Hellopeeps (Blue Dolphins), Hellopeeps (Gangster Squad), Hellopeeps (Groovy Group), Hellopeeps (McBursts), Hellopeeps (McBursts), Hellopeeps (Milly's Cheesy Moustaches), HHstarz, honey, horses!, IBBYFLOR, Ice Queen 24, ilovegreyhounds56, Isapop, Izthewiz (Teenyweeny IL), jamesbond (Teenyweeny EBP), Jedi 1, lemonfrosting, Lerwick Chatterbooks, Library Club, Lilazzyboomoo, Little Boot, little snout, London 2012, Love Labradors!, LPSsuperstar135, LucyLou, magicalsnowqueen, Manchester, Mario Kart Teenyweeny (JW), Marple Munchkins, meltedmarshmallows91569, Mertall$,

MickleﬁeldYear6Class, Mill and Joyce, millionstars, Miss Awesomeness 123, MJS Yr4 Reading Club, Monkey78, monster, netballfunny12, No1 girl (Teenyweeny SH), Obipower, Onedirection999 (Teenyweeny EJ), Owls, Pasta_lova12, pie123, pink cat, Pink panda, pixiedust12, Planet girl (Teenyweeny RR), ponylover, puppylove, PurplePuppy345, rainbow, ramsbottom, RockyBP, Rooster, RosePetals, RVProx, Sausage, sherbertgrape, shooting star, Silveryowl, Sketcher2000, Skulls07, Smiley2003, Snow leapords8, snow queen, snuffles, space girl, spiderman (Teenyweeny KM), Sri Lanka, St Peters 5, SuperGirl10, SweetCandy, SweetChoc, TargetBreakers, Teenyweeny, Teenyweeny (AC), Teenyweeny (AO), Teenyweeny (CC), Teenyweeny (JH), Teenyweeny (JN), Teenyweeny (JS), Teenyweeny (MK), Teenyweeny (PH), Teenyweeny (RT), Teenyweeny (SW), That-Creative-Boy, Theheart (Teenyweeny HH), tinkerbell, Titus, Twinkle, VLBellatrix, Weinbag, White wonder, Wonder Nerd, Year 6 Book Club, Year 6 Book Club (Babalix), Year 6 Book Club (Box of trix), Year 6 Book Club (Bubbleix), Year 6 Book Club (Coolix), Year 6 Book Club (Darlix), Year 6 Book Club (Geoix), Year 6 Book Club (Hoopix), Year 6 Book Club (Ickleix), Year 6 Book Club (Loopyix), Year 6 Book Club (Moonix), Year 6 Book Club (Oli-ix), Year 6 Book Club (Pick a mix), Year 6 Book Club (Robix), Year 6 Book Club (Sweetix), Year 6 Book Club (Tix), Year 6 Book Club (Tomix), Year 6 Book Club (Tomkix)

Discover more at hotkeybooks.com

[illegible]

14/5 BLOG

You Tube